# CLARKESW

CW01663837

## FICTION



## NON-FICTION




Neil Clarke: Publisher/Editor-in-Chief
Sean Wallace: Editor
Kate Baker: Non-Fiction Editor/Podcast Director

Clarkesworld Magazine (ISSN: 1937-7843) • Issue 211 • April 2024

# The Lark Ascending

## ELEANNA CASTROIANNI

They even took the violins. Every last one of them: Amadeus, Josephine, Mulberry, Nestor. They came into the house through the front door, guests without a host, a peculiar band of invited thieves. Plugged into my power station as a seemingly unthreatening household device, I watched them as they ransacked a life. They chatted and joked while scrubbing every nook and cranny, erasing every trace of Papa. They worked fast and efficiently. Within a single morning, nothing in the house would betray he ever lived there.

"Boss, what shall we do about this one? Protocol reset?" Sounded like it was his first day on the job.

Boss winced. "Nah, it's one of them," she said with a shake of her head. "Hestia's domestic helpers. Don't tamper with the software, ever. Not unless you want a letter before claim. They're ridiculously protective of their cute toys."

I stared sleepily through them, not uttering a word. Looking as cute and as toy-like as I could manage.

The young man shuffled his feet. He didn't seem convinced. I, too, was curious to learn more. Just letting me go like that sounded like a really sloppy job on their part. "Don't we need to be, you know . . . thorough?" Definitely his first day on the job. "This DH will still have memory of everything we cleared up, won't it?"

Boss sighed heavily and rolled her eyes. "You're new in this business. I forget." She pointed a finger at me. Rude. "Hestia DH run on independent protocols. We're not allowed to touch them. Every single one of them is logged and monitored because its parent company must send reports to the State. This one has probably already received the order to reset itself. They're extremely fast. In any case,"—Boss shrugged—"it's Hestia's responsibility, not ours. The only thing you should care about is that we've done our job. We're getting paid and no one can sue us."

The young man glanced at me one last time. "So there haven't been any problems with them at all?"

"None that I know of." Boss shook her head again in one swift motion. She was already walking out the door.

The moment they left I had just finished charging, the buzz of the plug a sharp, familiar sound.

Then silence. I stood there, waiting for Hestia's reset. Waiting and waiting. It didn't seem to come. Maybe it did arrive but something got away.

I could still remember everything.

On my little wheels, I rolled from room to room. Everything about Papa was gone.

Yet everything was somehow there, thickening the particles in the air like silica pumped full of moisture. When I saw the marks on the wall, I stopped my trek so abruptly I almost lost my balance.

One thing. One thing they missed. The marks on the wall: dashes made in ball-point pen, perpendicular to one imaginary line rising to heaven. The one thing only I would remember now. That's when I knew the marks would become a secret altar for me, the place where I would always stop to look.

We miss you, Papa.

The marks we leave behind are many, complicated, intertwined. They intersect other lines, leave echoes. How can you scrub a life off? The marks will still be on the wall. They might mean nothing to some, but they will mean everything to someone else.

It's just like the story of the rose and the bee Papa told you. I wonder: will you remember the story he told, if not him?

You arrive a week later, head still in bandages. "Tuki! Darling!" You pat my head. My name is still the one you gave me when you were too young. I watched you grow, become a new person every day. I've never stopped loving the name you gave me because it came from your lips.

"Welcome back. Are you feeling better, Pet?"

I stumble at my foolishness. I've said a word I shouldn't have said. They haven't reset me yet. If they're watching me, I might be in danger. But—I realize grimly—it flies right past your brand-new head.

"What are we having for dinner?" you say, as if nothing out of the ordinary happened. "Hospital food was horrible."

For a few seconds I stand still, my computation power strangely inadequate to elaborate on this reality. *Pet, darling, I made you spinach pie.* These words are etched in my long-term memory along with the image of Papa, affectionately spreading filo for you. Now they sound like some dream I conjured. "Your favorite, Pet," I say the word again, feeling bold. No reaction. They fixed you well. Too well. "Spinach pie."

We sit in silence, silence saying big words between us. Time passes and we receive guests. No family, because we don't have any. No friends, because all of them are either dead or missing. It's just the government inspectors who visit regularly, check in with you, with their psych and social worker and the subtle surveillance they're infamous for.

Daughter of an enemy of the State, but our Glorious Country is kind and gives opportunities to start anew. The social worker asks things like what your plans for the future are, what college would you like to go to. Beside her, the man with the invisible ennoblements is scanning the place. My aversion for the things—I, a completely artificial being of all beings—must have come from Papa. *Don't let them change you, Pet.* He knew the future was bleak, but he fought nevertheless. He taught you how to be a fighter too. Will you remember all this now? Is it, somehow, grafted into your skin, a legacy that's fused with your DNA just like an ennoblement, only better?

Hidden in the kitchen, I watch them, pretending hard to be just another appliance. Maybe I can get away with this. Maybe they will never know. I am not supposed to be smart after all—just cute and toy-like.

I am certain that his gaze crosses my own because I capture the magenta film flashing over his pupils. For a moment he stares at me, right through me—then his gaze wanders again.

He doesn't care—I'm harmless. And that's what I am, really. Even if I remember everything, what can I do?

Time passes and your hair grows long, a modern Rapunzel. Feet balancing weight between them, fingers twirling inside your locks, you ask me to cut your hair. But when I touch you, you burst in tears.

"Why am I crying, Tuki?"

I know why, but I am not allowed to say. So I say something else. Something I've heard before—something you've heard before. "I will cut your hair when you are ready. No one else needs to know."

Your face softens. *I will be Papa now,* a little voice inside me whispers. Almost spontaneously, as if programmed, I start to play music: *The Lark Ascending* by Ralph Vaughan Williams.

"I know this tune," you say from between your tears. Something like sunlight reaches your eyes.

For all their science, they made a mistake: people don't remember with their brains. Papa is everywhere around us, but he's screaming without a voice.

If you had the choice, would you have chosen it?

I was with Papa the night he was arrested. As always, everyone forgot about the Intelligent Non-Person household helper. They waited patiently for you to show up, welcomed you behind your own door with utmost kindness. "Your father will pay for his crimes against the State, but you can escape his fate," one of the agents said. He was beautiful and smartly dressed, had a wide, gentle smile. "There is a way to start anew."

"We saw that you are marked Gold in all the standardized school tests," the other agent explained. She was doll-like and just like a glossy movie star, her voice even showed admiration towards you. "Your school principal must have told you that you qualify directly for ennoblements. Your genetic potential is what we want for the future of this country. We are willing to forget your father's past, as long as you forget it too."

My memory of you that night seems peculiarly erased. I can't recall what you said or did. You were a blur against their eerie eyes and smiles, all designed in the same laboratory.

I don't know why they bothered explaining things to you; it was already decided, just like it always is with those things. I don't know if it was your father that pleaded them to spare you, even if that meant becoming part of what he hated—but I like to think that. And I like to think you'd never choose this. Perhaps it makes me feel better. What I know for sure is that you weren't given any choice, just like I wasn't.

You are stuck with forgetting; I with remembering.

He was a good papa. He raised you all by himself, playing bits of *The Lark Ascending* on Sunday mornings, marking your height progress on the wooden frame of the kitchen door: dashes made in ball-point pen, perpendicular to one imaginary line rising to heaven. He told you stories: "*Once upon a time, there was a little girl with curly hair . . . and her trusty friend was Tuki.*" He was the only one to ever cut your hair. Even when you were cured from psoriasis, you still wouldn't let anyone else touch your head.

Those were the moments that were still good, untarnished. By the time his drinking got worse, you were the adult. "I don't recognize you anymore," you said one evening. Those were my thoughts too, but no one asked me so I could never tell them. I had been watching him as he spiraled downwards, got sloppy with his missions, risked getting caught. All the while, there was nothing I could do.

Even now, my hands are tied.

When Papa found me, I was broken too. I was in the trash, stuck on a loop. "Why would anyone throw away such expensive, intelligent tech?" he kept asking his friend, not believing his luck in finding me. His tech-savvy friend was certain he could nurse me back to health. "It's an old model," he said as he soldered new life in me. Back then our house was full of people, coming and going. Friends, comrades. Printing pamphlets and planning sabotage. "Some people resell them, but this one broke so they just dumped it. Believe me, I can make it brand new. Your daughter will love it." This friend must have tampered with my protocols, cut me off from the parent company so no one could reset me when the time came—I simply went off the grid. I was rogue and I didn't even know it.

Indeed, Papa thought I'd be a good friend for you. "Take care of Pet," he instructed me once. "Her mother passed when she was too little. I'm not as strong as she was. One day, I'll get caught. One day, you'll take my place."

I could never guess my confusion at his change, those days when we couldn't recognize him. How can someone become another person? How could Papa hurt us so? Was grief what changed him? If so, isn't it better for Pet to forget him so that she, too, won't change?

What about me, then? Will I change? I run on algorithms and electricity: such a perfect imitation of organic-origin emotion. And yet, no one really knows what I'm like inside. No one knows how perfectly the imitation hurts either.

"Tuki. I think I'm forgetting something."

It's a quiet Sunday morning. I'm playing a recording of *The Lark*, very softly. It's a recording of Papa playing it with his favorite violin, Mulberry. If anyone's watching my processes, they won't know. I have renamed the file *Relaxing Forest Sounds*.

"I do not think you are forgetting anything, Pet." I mean it. Everything about the thing you've forgotten is here, with us. Even the grief of its absence. Especially that.

Your fingers tighten around your cup. There's something moving in the air between us. "Can't you talk to me about it?"

You're soon leaving for college. You're soon getting your first ennoblement: brain enhancements. You hope to work in tech, make things that improve people's lives.

I don't want to ruin it for you. I don't want to scare you off, simply because I worry that you'll become like the others, enhanced and arrogant. All I can hope for is that you've been raised well, to withstand and persevere, to retain your compassion, always. As I shape these thoughts, I know it's Papa's words that have shaped me too. He is everywhere around us, but he mostly lives in me.

"I cannot, Pet. But there is something I can do."

"What is it?"

"I can be a rose."

A flash of confusion, but perhaps something's there. "A what?"

I tell the story. A story you perhaps remember. "There is a rose that evolved to look appealing to a bee species. Its existence was, thus, shaped by the existence of the bee. Then the bee went extinct. The rose still bears the same shape. It still bears the marks of the bee's influence on its body. The existence of the rose still tells the story of the bee."

You blink at me, Papa's eyes staring out through yours. Somehow, you understand. "Why not cut my hair and tell me a story then?"

In this, I have a choice. A voice echoes inside me: *I will be Papa now.* Storytelling is not an art I've practiced much, but I've spent hours watching and listening to someone rather good at this.

I pull out my scissored limb. As it cuts across the first lock, you shiver. "There was a girl," I say, "with a blood ancestor and an intelligent non-person friend." The comforting sharp sound of cutting echoes in the room. In this, I can preserve the good memories. In this, I have a choice. "Let me show you the marks on the wall that signaled her growth progress."

## ABOUT THE AUTHOR

**Eleanna Castroianni** is a writer, poet and nomadic subject. A cultural geographer by training, Eleanna tells stories from the margins of history—a dark and mystical Greece marked by violence—and the far—or not so far—futures of capitalism and the Anthropocene. Eleanna's writing has appeared in *Beneath Ceaseless Skies, PodCastle, Fantasy Magazine, Fireside, The Stinging Fly, Strange Horizons,* and elsewhere. Lives in Athens, Greece with a growing number of string instruments.

# An Intergalactic Smuggler's Guide to Homecoming

TIA TASHIRO

There are seven hundred aliens hidden in Miko's backpack, and the Galactic Security Agent currently studying her passport (hopefully) has no clue. The agent is an alien themselves, some tentacular species with assistive devices hooked into its uniform to mist its soft skin every few seconds. A puff of evaporated solution exits from one of the devices by its neck as it draws her passport closer to its pitted eyes.

"You said you were coming from the X10-11 System," the agent rumbles. "Your stamp lists X10-10."

Miko shifts into the practiced lie, keeping her heart rate calm. She's heard some species working as GSA border authorities can sense minute changes in human physiology; she hopes this isn't one of them. "I ported through the X10-10 gate and starshipped over," she says. "X10-11 doesn't stamp you when ten already did."

The GSA agent considers her for a moment, and Miko tries to channel youth and innocence. Her dark hair is cropped short to her chin, in the fashion of a modern human teen, and tiny, stylish piercings sparkle along her eyebrows. By all accounts she looks just out of pre-uni, even if she's a decade older.

The GSA agent already swiped a scanner over her prosthetic hand and asked her if she had any prohibited or restricted items to declare, including but not limited to organic life, non-prescribed drugs, proprietary starship blueprints, unregistered AI systems, radioactive material, and fresh fruit. Miko, eyes wide, relinquished a cloverfruit from the X10 systems, apologizing profusely for not realizing it was classed as prohibited. She tripped over herself to explain that she "just wanted a snack on the ship!"

Let them get you for something small, and they don't think you'd dare with something big. Rina taught her that.

The agent reaches beneath their desk, and Miko smothers the urge to tense up. She's had a few close calls with forged documents. Once, it was only an opportune scanner glitch that saved her skin.

But the agent draws out a stamp, the pad glimmering with the signature nanotech embedded in the ink, and presses it down neatly on her passport. The GSA switched back to physical passports from digital after a cybersec scandal a decade ago—bypassing a scanner these days is tricky business. *Bypassing a person?* Miko thinks, satisfaction sinking in. *Not so much.*

The agent swipes a tentacle towards the door behind them. Down the line to Miko's left, dozens more GSA agents are doing the same, ushering immigrants and returning humans alike through to the spaceport. "Welcome back," the agent says, "to Terra Three starspace."

"Thanks," Miko says, giving them a little salute. And she doesn't even tremble when she passes the threshold to home.

In the backpack, where their tank presses against her spine, the seven hundred successfully smuggled aliens buzz with delight.

Miko's long and lucrative career in smuggling started on Terra Three. It was the third planet the humans had managed to terraform fully, and so it'd been done rather poorly—not with as much attention to detail as Terra One, nor as much experience and ingrained skill as the later iterations, Terra Five and above. Three was decidedly the middle child, created and forgotten.

It was smaller than most Terras, chosen for alteration back when humans thought that embedding gravity enhancers was a sustainable planetwide substitution for original mass. Later planetary engineers hadn't made the same mistake. Three's enhancers were always breaking down, requiring constant repairs just to keep gravity consistent.

Some countries on Three had abandoned their enhancers altogether, adjusting to lesser gravity despite the issues their citizens had with interplanetary travel. The intergalactic gravitation standard was much easier to handle without assistive devices when you grew up in an enhancer area, with its stronger, First Earth-equivalent pull.

The problem with Three being a backwater planet, half of it breaking down and the other half on the way, was that it meant it was a dead-end birthplace, too. Miko was born in a Three hospital with an assistive medsystem from a hundred years ago. She grew up a twin in a household packed with children, in a city packed with programmers, on a planet packed with people the galaxy didn't particularly care for.

Programming new tech for other Terras or fishing Three's vast seas paid enough to live on, so Miko didn't start smuggling because she needed money; she started smuggling because she needed out. Her planet was choking her. She'd decided at seventeen that she had to put herself first, and she didn't care what she had to leave behind. So just out of pre-uni, she'd hitchhiked up to orbit with a delivery crew and snagged a temp job working in the spaceport. She'd been there for two years when she found Sting and his crew over the livewire network.

It was a simple deal: do a job, get paid, travel. Do a bigger job, get paid more, travel further.

She'd started with small luxury items, ferrying expensive products between Terras. Then she'd upgraded into novelty drugs and illicit tech. She'd been in that arena for the last five years, and it was steady work. Sometimes, flipping between her passports in a pod hotel or shuttling goods through a far-flung spaceport, she forgot the desperation she'd felt on Three. The claustrophobia of knowing she was trapped on a backstage planet while the rest of the galaxy lived in the spotlight.

These days, she was selective with her jobs. She could afford to be; she didn't spend much on anything but travel, jetting from system to system in her time off. It scratched some itch in her soul, to settle into new gravities, flick her translator system into unfamiliar local tongues.

Sting had called her up about the seven hundred aliens when she'd been on vacation in Zeta-Pripoli, wandering through enormous coral forests and sipping down the neon pink drinks tagged acceptable for human consumption. (They tasted like a new passport smelled.)

Miko picked up his ping, easing back in her lounge chair in the warm orange light of Zeta-Pripoli's second sunset. Tiny fluttering aliens drifted past on the wind, tourists from another system. "Sting," she said, taking another sip of her drink, "don't you know it's rude to bother your runners during the holidays?"

"Don't be cute," Sting growled. He didn't mean to intimidate; she'd long since come to understand it was just the natural register of his voice, the way he sounded like he'd eaten a spoonful of sand and gotten it stuck in his throat. "I need you for a job."

She stirred her straw around the bottom of her glass, kicking up gauzy blue chunks of indeterminate origin. They tasted faintly of sea salt. "Get Leeo."

"Leeo got nabbed in a botched vapor job."

"Vapors?" Miko snorted. "He's getting sloppy."

"That's why I need you, doll. It's . . . delicate."

"Drugs?"

He hesitated—unusual, for Sting—then said, "Organics."

"You know I don't do corpses." They gave her the skives.

"They're not dead," Sting said. "Yet."

She didn't speak for a moment, choosing instead to fish out a sea salt chunk with her fingers and let it dissolve on her tongue. They both knew that meant she was leaning towards yes. She never could resist an interesting job.

"It's not trafficking, is it?" Miko had lines she wouldn't cross, and that was one of them. Sting wasn't clean by any means—she knew he handled drugs so damaging she wouldn't touch them, probably did things for bigger payoffs she'd be horrified to know about—but so far, it hadn't impacted their working relationship. He understood her boundaries.

He was good at compartmentalizing. So was she.

"I'll send you the listing," Sting replied, and cut the connection.

What came through to her livewire tablet was a message clearly decoded and fixed up by Sting's crew. It originated in the X10-11 system. Miko fished through her memory, and then, failing that, ran a quick tablet search. The primary habitable planet in eleven was populated by small lifeforms, each sentient perhaps only the size of her fingernail. The intelligent species called themselves the Xellia. The pictures she could find showed what looked like tiny jellyfish, pseudoneural connections gleaming through their translucent skin as they fired.

Some of the jellyfish had trailing tentacles of bioluminescent blue, some of matte aquamarine, others of a bruised purple. Apparently, the Xellia were waging an intraspecies war. The bioluminescent Xellia had been targeted and were being systemically destroyed. Because it was classed as intraspecies conflict, it didn't qualify for galactic intervention.

The bioluminescent Xellia were the ones who'd sent the message. They'd been blocked by hostile Xellia in their government from acquiring official travel certifications and were offering to pay anyone who'd be willing to get them off-planet.

It reminded Miko of her own escape from Three, though the Xellia were in much more dire straits. The message was less an advertisement and more a plea for help.

Sting was, unfortunately, right. The job was interesting. And the price tag the Xellia were offering for their safe rescue was well worth it, even if she factored in Sting's commission.

She pinged him a self-deleting text. "Send me the details."

• • •

Miko can relax a little now that she's back at Terra Three. The Xellia in her backpack are buzzing gently, a sign that they're communicating with each other. She can only imagine their relief.

The orbital station she's just entered is perpetually docked above Three. What with the unpredictable Three gravity enhancers, it's partially self-powered, with AI systems running the nuclear engines to help the station adjust to minute fluctuations in planetary gravity.

Miko pauses on a walkway in between a massive food court and a station segment filled with pod hotels. Nostalgia doesn't often prick at her, but maybe it's the Xellia's joy at being in Three starspace that encourages her to walk over to the porthole binos in the station wall and pay the credits for a two-minute glance at her homeworld.

She presses her face to the bino's metal, shiny from thousands of humans who've done the same before her. Through the lenses, she can see Three, the enormity of its body moving beneath the ever-falling station.

The continents and poles couldn't be more different from the First Earth maps she and Rina memorized together in ancient history class. There are three large landmasses and countless small islands freckling the rest of the planet's surface. Swirling clouds, bringing weather patterns she remembers but can't name, sweep across the area. The great majority of the planet's surface is ocean; apart from the programmers, Three's economy is bolstered by the export of seafood. The planet is basically an enormous fish farm.

She'll be meeting Sting down there tomorrow, in the warren of apartments and sentients that makes up Eldern City, when she delivers the Xellia and gets paid. Miko only handles the smuggling. The rest is Sting's problem.

Sting's based out of Three for a reason. As far as dead-end planets go, illicit operations on Three don't get much attention from the authorities—unlike, say, Terra Two, which is notorious for both crackdowns on illegal activity and the mysterious deaths of arrested parties in the aftermath. No wonder Sting prefers Three.

Miko figures he'll probably forge travel documentation for the Xellia after she drops them off, bringing the job full circle. Or, for an easier option, help them apply for asylum with galactic officials.

The binos cut off, hitting their time limit, and Miko draws back from them. Hefting the backpack higher on her shoulders, she makes for the hotel area to rent a pod for the night. And the station around her falls, falls, falls.

• • •

The pickup was easier than Miko imagined. She had arrived on X10-11 by starship from X10-10, carefully avoiding being tagged as a foreigner too far removed from their neighbor systems. X10-11 was a low-hospitality system for a human, but there were a few human-friendly hotels on the primary planet.

She met her contact there, a small alien with fat deposits layered heavy on their limbs and a proboscis that scented the air when she walked in for the handoff. The hotel room was small, clearly built for function over luxury; thin transparent pipes threaded down the hallways and past the door, and she'd caught glimpses of Xellia swimming through them.

Her contact passed the backpack on to her, sending a proximity message to her tablet. *Can't talk here*, they wrote. *Package contains the goods. Leave via X10-10.*

*Confirmed*, she replied, the prosthetic finger of her right hand clicking against her tablet screen. *Thanks, friend.*

The alien fixed her in the doleful gaze of its single large eye. She got the sense it didn't consider them friends.

With an awkward salute, she slung the backpack over her shoulders and left the way she'd come.

In the Three hotel pod, having paid an extra fee for a secure room, Miko sets the backpack gently on the bed and unzips it. It isn't that she doesn't trust Sting, but they're working with organics, and that warrants a level of caution she doesn't normally bother with.

As soon as the zipper cracks, a warm blue glow billows out from the backpack. She pulls it open to reveal a flexible, transparent tank of seven hundred Xellian escapees, their bioluminescent tendrils flickering in the low light of the pod room.

They're so small, smaller than the pictures made them seem. Curls of red rest in their jellyfish-esque bodies, like tiny, twisted hearts—though Miko wouldn't make the mistake of assuming their anatomy is comparable to any other sentient's.

In unison, they pulse towards her, and the buzzing she's felt against her back finally gains form. She reaches for the hearing aid in her right ear and clicks on her translator system. She downloaded Xellian back on Zeta-Pripoli as soon as she took the job. She presses a speaker patch to the Xellia's tank to relay her responses to them.

The buzzing coalesces into understandable speech. "Thank you," the Xellia are saying, "thank you!"

Miko suppresses a smile, a surprising warmth in her cheeks. "It's just a job," she replies, her words turning to a static buzz against the tank. "You paid well."

She's not used to her cargo's gratitude, but then, she's never smuggled sentients before. The Xellia pulse up and down in unison, swarms of them breaking off and rejoining the main cluster as they listen to the translation. "We would have died," they say in response. "You cannot pay too much for a life."

The words strike truer than Miko thinks they could've imagined. That's one thing she's learned in her galactic travels. You can replace a dead starship, tablet, gravity enhancer: it doesn't matter. Those things don't gather experience like cobwebs in the corners of minds. It has never ceased to amaze Miko how irreplaceable sentients are. There is no way to perfectly replicate the unique cocktail of experience each sentient brings to the universe. Even a genetic clone raised in near-perfect symmetry to its DNA donor will diverge in minute, unpredictable ways. It is a kind of magic.

Miko knows this more intimately than most. Rina, her twin, lives somewhere in Eldern City, one of the many things Miko gave up chasing the stars. The only one of those many things she regrets.

She pinches down the residual shame. The Xellia are right; you can't pay too much for a life. Maybe it's a sign for Miko to start mending bridges, reach back out to the sister she sacrificed for her freedom. Maybe she'll ping Rina when she has delivered the Xellia to Sting.

Or maybe not, because the idea of looking Rina in the eye after all these years has Miko cringing in imagined discomfort.

She shakes herself out of it and strikes up a conversation with the smuggled Xellia. She learns about their planet, their names, their traditions. She learns that, like humans, they were mislabeled as a hive species when accepted into the galactic registry of sentients—though unlike humans, they haven't yet gotten the designation removed. She learns that now that they're safe, some of them want to go back for their fellows, get alterations to disguise their bioluminescence so they can fake documentation for their friends. Some of them want to petition for galactic intervention despite the intraspecies clause.

"We could use your help," the Xellia venture, when the rapport between them has set down tentative roots. "Your skills, your knowledge."

Miko laughs. "Me? Sorry, but no. Someday I'll get out of this business, but for now I'll keep my head down. The money's good." It's not just that. Miko's good—no, *great*—at her job. She's had a longer career than a lot of runners. She attributes this to a combination of skill and luck. The skill, for the moments when she chats her way through a checkpoint or ditches a package just before she would've been caught with it, primed to be picked up later. The luck, for the near misses—like that time when a security agent's tablet alerted at her forged documents before they refreshed their system and the alarm disappeared. She'd thought she was done for. Sting told her a year or two back that she must have had a guardian angel, to not yet be in prison or dead. She took it as a compliment.

"And you like this life?" the Xellia ask. She's surprised at how polite they manage to sound in their collective voice.

Miko shrugs. "I like what it gives me. Credits in my account, a chance to explore. I have things—people—that I miss. But . . . I don't think they miss me." That statement—it sounds pathetic, really—hangs in the air for a few moments, punctuated only by the gentle buzzing of the Xellia listening and her tablet display flickering the way it sometimes does, an occasional glitch in tech she's had since she lived on Three. A glitch that Rina could've fixed.

Miko swallows, tugging herself out of her own head. "You mentioned a festival, earlier, for the movement of the tides on your planet. Can you tell me more?"

The Xellia surge forward into the new topic, perhaps sensing her reticence to linger on the old one. Miko lies back on the pod bed and talks with her cargo deep into the night, their glow pulsing against the walls. It intrigues her that she's spent so much time in the far reaches of the galaxy, and yet, miles above the surface of her home planet, she's still learning something new.

Miko and Rina were inseparable until Rina discovered computers. Before that, Miko had been the one to range out from the cramped apartment their extended family shared, swimming in Eldern Bay and dreaming of worlds beyond Three. Rina had always tagged along, joining in on Miko's adventures as readily as her aspirations. Side by side, they'd gotten into trouble and weaseled out of it again.

But then they'd grown into school, and Rina had fallen in love with her hands on a tablet and eyes on a screen.

Rina was a brilliant programmer. And suddenly, she didn't much care about travel; she didn't much care about getting out. She cared about her tablet and about Miko, and sometimes Miko didn't know which of the two would've come first if it came down to bare wires.

Still, when Miko dreamed out loud at dinner about getting off-planet, Rina always nodded along. When she talked about getting a job on a starship as soon as she was of age, Rina kept promising to snag a position, too. When she and Rina worked at the docks in the busy season helping their uncles and aunts load their hauls into transport crates, they commiserated and took solace in the fact that they'd someday leave the stench of fish on Three and jet off into the stars.

And then when Miko was seventeen, Rina got a deal with a top programming firm on Three, and all Miko's plans came crashing down when her twin said she was taking it. Where were the whispered promises, the shared dreams, the staunch loyalty of sisters?

They'd gotten into an argument that morphed quickly into a shouting match. Well, shouting on Miko's part—it was almost worse that Rina hadn't raised her voice, not even by the end.

"Of course I'm staying," Rina had said, craned over her tablet. She'd barely looked at Miko the whole argument, just cut disapproving glances at her when she'd yelled—glances that said, *can't you see? I'm working.* She'd been that way for months, too absorbed by her tech to pay Miko any mind. "I've said all there is to say. There's a path for me here. Opportunities. I can't give that up for a pipe dream, and you won't, either. You wouldn't do that to me."

Miko had spent the last half hour begging Rina not to do that to *her*. A whole galaxy that didn't give a damn about Miko, and now her own sister was treating her the same.

"When I'm gone," Miko spat, pressing her toes against the rim of the threshold, "don't bother reaching out."

Rina snorted. "I'll see you at the docks tomorrow."

Miko opened her mouth. Closed it. Balled up her feelings and shoved them in some dark compartment in the corner of her mind.

She shouldered her bag, turned away, and left without a word.

She was in orbit by the next morning.

The audacity of Rina, to act like Miko leaving would be a betrayal. Only one twin had abandoned the other, and it hadn't been Miko.

That was when Miko realized she had to put herself first. When she decided she didn't care what she had to leave behind. That was the mindset she'd held for two years before she met Sting, clutching independence like a religion.

The orbital elevator from the station down to Three takes Miko, her backpack, and the Xellia hidden inside to a transit hub just east of Eldern. The Xellia buzz friendly in the pack; now that the border crossing is over, Miko feels comfortable leaving on her translator. Connected to the speaker patch, it pipes the Xellia's words into her ear in a low hum of conversation as she swipes her pass to get into the maglev station.

It only takes an hour to get to Eldern. Miko hasn't been back for years; she usually makes her handoffs at Sting's request, pinged remotely. Today, however, is a direct delivery. She understands the caution around this job, with what the Xellia are paying.

She messages Sting when she passes the outskirts of the city, the cycler yards that handle the massive amounts of waste produced by the programming hub. He pings her with a location, a self-deleting text; he keeps moving to avoid any potential authorities getting on his trail.

The location is down by the docks, and it's a nice enough day she decides to leg it. The sky is tinted blue by atmosphere, and clouds that remind her of Xellian tentacles brush against the skyscrapers. Miko hooks her prosthetic thumb under the right strap of her backpack and tilts her gaze down to the ground. She looks different, and the city is big, and none of that stops her from worrying she'll be recognized.

She makes it to the location without incident. She takes the stairs up, like Sting taught her—more exit paths that way—and knocks at the door.

The apartment is empty but for a table and a few black bags in one corner. The patterned wallpaper is peeling at the edges, revealing the gray synthesized materials underneath. It smells faintly of fish. It gives her the skives, and she can't quite place why.

There's one other man in the room besides Sting, with features she's seen once but can't quite pin down, like a word on the tip of her tongue. The hair raises at the back of her neck. She doesn't like the way he carries himself, but if he's Sting's, Miko won't question it.

Sting's a slim man, the shape of his cheekbones obvious under his sallow skin. It's been a while since she saw him in person; he looks older, wrinkles crinkling the corners of his eyes. He grins at her, which is unusual until she realizes he's grinning at the backpack. He gestures at the table, and she sets it down gently, trying not to disturb the Xellia inside. They've fallen quiet. She thinks they're probably listening.

"Any trouble with customs?"

Miko shakes her head. "Pulled the cloverfruit trick."

"And that's why you're my best runner, doll. You keep your cool, you think on your feet, you do what you have to do. I value that, Miko, I really do. Just a moment, and I'll get you paid."

He unzips one corner of the backpack, confirms the contents, and grunts in satisfaction, just like it's a normal package from one of his runners. He pulls his tablet from his pocket. In a few moments, hers pings; she checks it to see he's deposited her take for the job.

"That'll be all, Miko," he says, giving her a little salute. "Appreciate your work, as always. I'll be in touch."

It's clearly a dismissal, but a memory is niggling at Miko's mind. The man in the corner is looking at the glow of the Xellia in a way she doesn't like.

She should leave. She should just go. She doesn't care what Sting does after she finishes her part of the job. She's good at compartmentalizing. Isn't she?

"Wait," she says. She points at the man in the corner. "What's he doing here?" The memory resolves itself, just enough for her to see the edges. "Isn't he one of your pharma guys?" Her tone is light, curious, nonconfrontational. It doesn't betray the shiver going down her spine, the sense that something's wrong.

"Oh, yeah," Sting says casually, turning back towards the table. "Flynn's been doing some research. Turns out the cargo's chock full of a potent psychoactive. Luxe stuff, ten times better than vapors, worth a fortune. Might have you run it for me when he's done with the distillation."

Miko hopes he isn't saying what she thinks he's saying. "It's illegal to harvest controlled substances from sentients," she says, tone still light.

He laughs. "It's illegal to smuggle sentients too, doll. Look, if it's really eating at you, I'll drop a few extra credits in your account after the sale. Nobody's going to miss them. Who even gives a damn about X10-11?"

Nobody. Nobody cares about X10-11, just like nobody cares about Terra Three, just like nobody cares about all the little people doing their best to survive, to get free.

But this isn't Miko's problem. She doesn't owe the Xellia anything. They knew the risks, reaching out on the dark side of the network like they did.

She has to put herself first. She has to leave them behind. Those extra credits will buy her passage back to Zeta-Pripoli to get smashed on as many of those little pink drinks as she wants.

She wonders if it's the Xellia's tentacles that contain the drug Sting wants, or if it's embedded in the jelly of their flesh, or if it's what colors the red of their tiny, twisted hearts. She thinks of talking late into the night, the static of their language full of hopes and dreams.

She's been working for Sting for eight years. She's his best runner. He trusts her. That's the only reason this handoff is so relaxed. The only reason she has a chance.

"Sting?" Miko says, shifting onto the balls of her feet.

"Yeah, doll?"

"I quit."

With one explosive motion, the power driven by a childhood of swimming in the bays and the knowledge that you won't break a prosthetic hand on someone else's nose, Miko punches Sting full in the face and grabs for the backpack. She doesn't stop to assess the damage or let the weight of what she's done hit her like double-grav. She bolts.

She's fast, and scared, and she takes the stairs two at a time as she flies downwards. She barely pauses to pull a fire alarm on the wall as she goes. The bells ring loud and insistent in her ears, and she thinks of the elevators stuttering to a halt. As she barrels out onto the street, she catches shouts of pursuit mingling with the alarm.

But Three is still her homeworld, and Eldern City is still her birthplace. Miko knows the city down to its DNA. She threads her way through back alleys and under docks, dodges drones and evades security, and finally, finally, locks herself into the restroom of a twenty-four-seven party bar too full of music and lights to notice one sweating escapee.

She sits on a toilet lid and presses her forehead to the backpack, perspiration dampening her hair. Her eyebrow piercings click against the zipper.

"Oh, shit," she says, closing her eyes. The words echo against the smooth tile of the bathroom. "Oh, *shit*."

But the curse doesn't come out with as much fervor as she expected, and she realizes she's gasping in a sort of high-pitched, hyperventilating giggle. She unzips the backpack just enough to check that the Xellia are still there, still alive. Their tiny bioluminescent tentacles blink at her in confirmation. Miko laughs, again, louder this time. And she can't find it in herself to be sorry.

She checks her prosthetic. It's undamaged from the strike.

Sting will make it hard to get off-planet. He'll probably put a bounty on her head. Maybe he'll consider her record of services rendered and forgive her the indiscretion of punching him in the face, but she wouldn't bet on it.

Still. Didn't Sting himself once say it's like Miko has a guardian angel? Isn't she luckier than most? Her family's still on Three, *Rina's* still on Three, but Miko wouldn't drag them into her current situation for a trillion credits. So it's just her and the Xellia. She can't rely on anyone else. They've got a chance, slim as it may be.

She has plenty of experience smuggling things. She hopes she'll be able to handle smuggling herself.

There's no shot at the orbital elevator. If Miko knows Sting, he has eyes on the cameras and a few lackeys on foot, making sure to cover their bases even if she somehow manages to loop the feeds. She could try her luck on a charter shuttle, but she'd guess he's covering those just as thoroughly. If she were Sting, she'd have eyes on anything with a pulse headed into orbit.

Which is why Miko and the Xellia are currently crammed into a banged-up transport crate in one of the minor fishing conglomerate's delivery shuttles. It's the same standardized crate Miko slung thousands of fish into during the busy season as a teen, helping her family earn out their catch. A functioning crate would freeze the contents automatically when the lid shut, to be weighed and paid out once it arrived at its destination.

A *non*-functioning crate—like the ones Miko and Rina used to play in despite their parents' scoldings, or the one Miko is currently inside, swiped from where it was tagged for waste pickup by the docks—has a broken cooling element. And the ability to be rigged up so it gets enough airflow for, say, one human to survive.

Miko is, for all intents and purposes, currently registering as a very large dead fish. No pulse to speak of.

The worst of the experience thus far was the nauseating sway when the AI engine of an automated forklift identified her crate as belonging to its shuttle and lifted her into its bay. It was an unpleasantly disorienting experience: the beeping of the forklift coming from just outside the crate, the unpredictable movement as it set her down, the heavy scent of rotten fish permeating her erstwhile sanctuary. But she's alive, and so are the Xellia, and as they are all pressed downwards as the shuttle lifts off, she hears the Xellia whispering encouragements in her ear.

Miko closes her eyes, trying not to be sick.

Over the past few days, she's ditched most of her belongings. All she has now are the clothes on her back, the Xellia, and her tablet.

She's not an idiot—the tablet didn't have any location tracking hardware in the first place, and its network connection routes through dozens of systems, rendering it untraceable—but she's weighed her options, and the benefits of keeping the tablet outweigh the risks. That tablet, clutched in her sweaty hand, is her last resort. It hosts a data bundle developed over eight years, containing the intimate details of a vast, multi-system smuggling operation—though if asked, she of course wouldn't know anything about that.

She's good at compartmentalizing. That doesn't mean she didn't pay attention to how, where, and with whom Sting does business. Another thing you learn on a homeworld where gravity craps out at random? It never hurts to have insurance.

She hopes she won't need it.

The claustrophobic ascent is, thankfully, short. Miko feels the docking of the shuttle, a clunk that reverberates through the ship and the crate as it locks in. Then, voices. The Xellia fall silent.

She is out of her element, now. She knew well enough what happened to the crates on the ground; but when they reach the spaceport? This is new territory. She was hoping that it'd be a bot system unloading the cargo, that she could wait until she was moved and then pop out and run while it was reaching for the next crate. But those are human voices.

She hears a low mechanical *beep*, distant from her crate. One more, then another. *Are they moving closer?*

And then someone speaks, and she recognizes the voice.

A runner. One of Sting's. Newer than Miko, and Miko only remembers the voice because it's slightly nasal. The end of every sentence tilts upwards, like a question.

*Beep.* "Natch," the runner says. *Beep, beep.* "Nope. Nada."

"Could you *possibly* speed things up?" A second voice says. "We're meant to be on our way to Four by now, and you people—"

"Are the kind of people you don't want on your bad side," the runner drawls. "Trust me, I have better places to be than scanning a pile of postmortem seafood, too."

Miko's worse than a sitting duck; she's a sitting duck with seven hundred aliens relying on her to save them, and also a tremendous back cramp from being curled inside a fish crate.

The beeping approaches. So do the footsteps. Miko holds her breath.

*Beep, beep, beep.* "Nope, nope, nope," the runner says, so close Miko can hear her hiss through her teeth as she taps the crate directly to Miko's left. "Waste of time," she mutters.

The runner will have a weapon, and Miko's unarmed, hemmed in. A thousand possible futures all lead to her and the Xellia dead, here and now, because Sting was one step ahead of her.

*Bleeep.*

"Damn thing," growls the runner. "Lost signal." Miko nearly jumps out of her skin as something taps on her crate, just above her head. The scanner emits a low whir, then a cascade of cheery burbles. "And . . . we're back," the runner says. "Joy."

Miko closes her eyes, waits for the end.

*Beep.*

"Natch," says the runner, and keeps moving.

Thirty-four minutes later, when the voices have faded out and Miko's heart has stuttered back to a semi-regular rhythm and the shuttle has started moving again—now, she surmises, heading to Four—she gets a ping on her tablet. It's a familiar ID, albeit unexpected.

> *Fish crate, huh? Creative. Glad I had eyes on the shuttles.*

Miko stares at the ID, glowing from the screen in the dark of the crate. She rubs her eyes with her free hand. When the ID doesn't change—suggesting that hallucination is out of the question—she taps out a response.

> *Rina, what the hell.*

She considers this, then adds three exclamation points. For the first words she's exchanged with her sister in years, she supposes she could've been more eloquent, but she still feels the ghost of Sting's breath on the back of her neck. Further—as the rest of Rina's message sinks in—Miko doesn't *understand.*

> *How do you know about the fish crate?*

> *I spoofed the results on the scanner that woman was using,* Rina messages. *Dead fish all the way down.* A few seconds later, she adds, *Don't be mad.*

Miko curls tighter around the Xellia, taking comfort from their humming. She swallows, then messages, *You helped me?*

> *It wasn't the first time. Look, let me keep this short. I know we didn't leave on good terms. I get if you don't want anything to do with me. And this isn't meant to make you feel like you owe me anything, really, I know you'd hate that. I just want you to be safe. So . . . you died in jail twenty minutes ago.*

Miko blinks at her screen. *I did WHAT?*

> *You got off Three unnoticed, but you were picked up by Two's law enforcement while trying to make a changeover in Terra Two starspace,* Rina writes. *We all know what they're like, don't we? You were found dead in your cell while awaiting trial. So sad.*

> *You faked my death?*

> *Wasn't hard. Terra Three programmers like me built Two's systems, Miko. A few falsified forms won't raise any eyebrows, and even if one of your old crew has a mind to keep digging, they'll have plenty on their hands soon enough. You'll never guess what those Two officers found on your tablet. That was some quality dirt, by the way. Proud of you. In my line of work, we appreciate good documentation.*

Miko types a response, erases it, types it again. By then, Rina has messaged one more line.

> *You'll have a window when you land on Four, based on the shuttle schedules. Thirty minutes after landing before they unload the bay. Like I said. You don't owe me. You don't have to talk to me. But if you change your mind, I'm here. Ping me, okay?*

Miko sends the message. *When did you start paying attention?*

> *Miko, really?* Rina replies. *I never stopped.*

And with that, Miko's tablet goes dead.

Curled up in the dark, she thinks about Rina's message: *It wasn't the first time.*

"She was there," Miko whispers to the Xellia, pressing her hand against her translation patch. "She thought I didn't want her to, because of what we—what I said, when I left her on Three."

Sting once said Miko had a guardian angel. All those tiny hints—the security agent's disappearing alert, the scanner against the crate, maybe even her flickering tablet screen—avalanching into a truth. "She didn't leave me," Miko says. "She wants me to be safe. She . . . she *cares.*"

"Who?" the Xellia whir, humming against Miko's palm.

"My sister," Miko says, feeling the future unfurl before her. "Who else?"

A world away, a man with a purpling bruise high on his cheekbone examines a Terra Two mugshot on his tablet screen. That familiar jagged hairstyle. Those stupid eyebrow piercings.

"Got off Three, and that's a hell of a thing." Sting sighs. "But the luck runs out for all of us, doll. At least I didn't have to do it, yeah?" He brushes his thumb against his bruise and gives the picture a grudging nod.

Then he starts sending out pings, calling off the search. This whole matter has been bad for business.

Three weeks later, on a distant planet in a distant system, a woman with hair recently shaved to her scalp and sunglasses settled on her nose (totally unrelated to any concerns about the identifiability of her prior hairstyle and facial piercings) bids farewell to a group of small, bioluminescent sentients. They're officially registered as asylum seekers in the greater galaxy, as of a few days ago.

The static buzzes against her translator. "You'll be all right," the Xellia murmur, a promise to themselves as much as her. They've been worrying over her since Three.

"So will you," she says, forcing a smile. "And hey, you're going to miss your transport if you don't get a move on."

"Until we meet again," the Xellia whir, and she feels a pang of loneliness as she detaches the translator patch.

It won't be a goodbye forever—she's decided to take them up on their offer and work by their side, once she's gotten enough modifications to fool any facial recognition systems she might otherwise trip. She'll help them go back for their family, their friends. But for now, she'll lay low and give news of her death time to spread.

Miko finds a beach and a human-friendly café and orders a drink. She takes it to a small, private corner of blue sand, tucking herself under the eaves of a spreading umbrella. The sunlight glittering off the water is beautiful. The drink is strong and smooth. She realizes she's looking forward to the career change.

There's a lot of freedom in the business of being dead.

And there's someone she could thank for that.

Part of her still flinches when she thinks of Rina. It's an automatic response, from a painful memory revisited so often she's massaged it into the contours of her brain. It would take a long time to weave back together what they once had. Even longer, to spin the fragile thread of something new.

Her sister at seventeen, brow furrowed, eyes latched to a tablet screen. Dismissal dripping from her tongue. Betrayal, thick in Miko's throat.

A guardian angel, protecting Miko through the furthest reaches of space. Following her to the stars. In a way, a promise kept.

*You don't owe me,* Rina wrote. *You don't have to talk to me. But if you change your mind, I'm here.*

Miko pulls out her new tablet, hesitates for only the briefest of moments in her messaging system, and sends her sister a ping.

## ABOUT THE AUTHOR

**Tia Tashiro** is a multiracial speculative fiction writer hailing from the Pacific Northwest. By day, she works in a neurobiology lab; by night, she writes; and in between, she dabbles in stained glass and juggling, though never at the same time. Her short fiction is published in *Clarkesworld* and forthcoming in *Apex* and *Uncanny.*

# The Indomitable Captain Holli

## RICH LARSON

Holli was hanging upside down off the edge of her flimsy folding bed, watching goretoons in her goggles, when Puck the Pirate showed up again.

*Ahoy, Holli! Guess what?* His red-cheeked puppet face swelled, blocking out the show, which annoyed Holli until his next words. *Today's the Big Day!*

She twisted upright and yanked her goggles down, earpods popping free with them, to make sure she was alone in the apartment. She saw bumpy white walls, a big slab table, a floor scattered with garbage.

No Mama, because Mama was still at the fab. No big sister, because Estima was still somewhere with Lemar, even though she swore Lemar was not her boyfriend and double-swore she would kill Holli if Holli kept whispering Lemar's name in her ear.

Holli pulled the goggles back on. "The day we go all the way to the top of the Block?"

*Aye, aye, Holli.* Puck's mouth clacked up and down. *Tip-top, tippity-top! That's where the pirate party happens! Are you ready?*

Holli hesitated, sticking her hand down the back of her fraying fab-pants. "My bum and my asshole is itchy," she said. "Do you have a bum and an asshole, Puck?"

Puck's high-pitched laugh burbled through her earpods. *Of course. And they're stinky, stinky, stinky.*

Holli giggled in her throat. "You're funny, Puck."

*So are you, Holli. We'll have lots of funny fun together. Are you ready to go?*

Holli took her hand back out to chew at the skin between her thumb and pointer finger. She was bored, and Puck was fun, and they had talked lots of times about the Big Day. But she still felt a little wriggle in her belly. A little scaredy-worm wriggle.

"Show me the map again," she suggested.

Puck's face dissolved into a picture of the Block, but from the outside, how drones saw it. Her home was big, taller than all the smashed-up ruins around it, maybe even taller than the moon. There was only one other thing in the city near the same size. She rotated the view, and shivered.

"I know what that other tower is," Holli said. "That's the Bad Block. They got no eyes, and Estima says the mamas and dadas eat their kids. The mamas pick the best one and boil them and they make soup. And the dadas say, ooh, good soup, good soup."

*Good soup!* Puck agreed, putting on a rumbling dada voice. *Holli soup is good soup for me! Now look.*

Puck zoomed in, to show the Block's honeycombed insides. She saw her own little apartment, blinking red, and then the path Puck wanted her to take, way up past the hydrofarms and past the fabs and past the flesh-factory. She had never gone so high in the Block, and never ever on her own.

"It's far," she said. "I'll get tired." She stomped her feet in slow motion. "Tired, tired, I'm so tired . . . "

*It's far because it's an adventure*, Puck said. *A pirate adventure! Look, your hands are hooks.*

Holli glanced down through her goggles and saw her hands had turned into shiny sharp hooks. "Make them purple," she suggested. "No. Make them orange and purple."

The hooks changed color, pale purple with blots of orange—her favorite combination.

She snarled and swung them around. "Good," she said. "I like these hooks. You have hooks, too, Puck?"

*I have hooks and I have lines and I have lures,* Puck said, which wasn't as funny as his usual jokes. *Now it's time to get going, Holli the Stinky Purple Pirate. Out the door!*

Holli hopped all the way up to it, waving her hooks, before she remembered. "Can't open the door," she said, with a sort-of-sad, sort-of-glad feeling. "Mama did a new hacklock, and Estima won't teach me, so I can't open it until Mama's back from the fab."

Puck's grin didn't change. *Oh, I think today you can, Holli. If you just wish hard enough!*

Holli frowned. "I'm wishing," she lied.

*Today you can do a lot of things,* Puck said. *You know why?*

There was a buzzing clank, and suddenly all the lights went off, plunging the apartment black. Through the walls she heard grinding and sparking, electricity noises. Distant sirens started to drone.

Holli watched with mingled terror and delight as the door swung open. A blinking blue trail appeared in her goggles, ushering her out into the gloomy hall.

"Today's the Big Day," she muttered. She took a deep breath and skipped off into the dark.

The bugbear emerged from the maintenance shaft on Strip 36, a slice of old habitation units clammed between airfacs and derelict recreation pods. Its compound eyes rendered the dark corridor in infrared: bruise blue swatched with blots of orange and yellow, residual heat from the dead electric grid.

No visible threats, but pawn sounds echoed on all sides. The bugbear processed the voices for tonality, vocabulary, and deemed them hostile. It readied the needles in its maw, one with a precise dose of ketamine, the others with standard neurotoxin. Then an old decision tree budded anew and sent it to the ceiling, choosing witness evasion over witness elimination.

The bugbear set off upside down, pneumopods sucking softly at concrete. When it dropped down at the prescribed location, it found the door already open. The bugbear was not capable of feeling surprise, but the conflict of projection and reality set off a cascade of error potentials as it slipped inside the cramped apartment.

Traces of the target were everywhere. Dead skin and sweat stains on the bed, screaming with its tantalizing genes. A smear of shit on the toilet seat, teeming with its unique gut flora. All the identifiers the bugbear had imprinted six hours ago.

The target itself was nowhere. Normally the bugbear would have shuttled this projection-reality discrepancy to its owner for full reassessment, but those functions had been locked seven hours ago. On the Opponent's territory, any foreign outgoing signal would burn like a flare and draw reprisals.

Fortunately, the bugbear was equipped for improvisation. It padded to the door, following a faint waft of the target's molecular signature, and began its hunt.

Estima had been about a Planck time away from her second-ever orgasm when the electricity cut out, turning the warm sweaty bodies around her back into gray polygons. Lemar yanked his fingers free with a surprised yelp, and Estima felt the ragged slicy edge of a nail, which made her howl and slam one of her kneecaps into Lemar's chin, and it was all ruined.

She wrestled her goggles off. "What the *fuck*, Lemar."

"Same to you." Lemar's voice was sulky. "You cracked me in the jaw."

The utility closet they'd lovingly swathed in soft pink insulation and lit with scavenged fiber optics was now pitch dark, and judging by the way Lemar was scrabbling at the door, it was also sealed shut. Estima's legs steadied, and the last of the fizzing sparking gush in the bottom of her belly trickled away, leaving only the sting.

"You sliced my vag with your fingernail," she snapped.

"Shit." Lemar stopped scrabbling, and she could almost hear the blood rushing to his face. "Shit. Sorry. Is it bad?"

Estima tipped her head back and probed around the cut. "Dunno," she said. "I can't tell if it's bleeding or what." She found her scrunched underwear in the corner and started pulling them gingerly back on. "Why you so jumpy? It's just load shedding."

"Our strip wasn't supposed to be load shedding today," Lemar muttered. "Listen. It's the emergency siren."

Estima listened, and heard the faint electric wail. Her gut curled.

"Maybe it's an attack," Lemar said, in his half-joking voice. "Maybe the Bad Block finally got up the gall."

"It's our own custodians glitching out," Estima said, and by reflex added the old rhyme, the one her ma used to say when things in the centuries-old Block went haywire. "Machine error, no need for terror."

"But Holli's alone, so she's probably bad scared." Lemar made a motion that was probably him rubbing his chin. "You were meant to be watching her, right?"

"She's not scared of anything," Estima said, tamping down a small surge of guilt. "She's a little psychopath." She fingered the dead lenses of her goggles. "But if her goretoons quit, she's going to get bored and tear the whole apartment to shreds."

"And if your ma gets back before you do, she's wilding." Lemar slammed his bony shoulder against the door again. "And if your ma tells mine—"

"Here, budge over," Estima said, heart pumping hard again, this time with the bad kind of adrenaline. "Let me get at the locking pad."

Holli was walking backwards, partly to practice and partly to annoy Puck, who was in a big hurry to get to the hydrofarms. The dark made it extra exciting, like she was maybe going to step backwards off the edge of a chasm and go splat like a spagbag at the bottom.

She could hear people shouting and cursing from inside their apartments, and babies squalling, and that was exciting too. The neighbors were all locked up—*toss 'em in the brig*, Puck said—and she had free run of the whole strip, maybe even the whole Block. It made her feel all floaty and giggly.

*Do you still like climbing things, Holli?* Puck asked in her goggles.

"I like walking backwards," Holli said. She stumbled as she said it, and glanced over her shoulder to make sure she wasn't going to bash into the concrete wall.

*Good pirates have to climb things!* Puck said. *They go up up up the mizzenmast, into the crow's nest!*

"What's a crow's nest?" Holli demanded, arms out for balance.

*What's a mizzenmast?* Puck demanded back. *Nobody knows! Take a left, Holli. Left, left, left.*

Holli ran into the wall and thumped down hard on her tailbone. "Ouch!" she shouted. "You tricked me, Puck."

*Right and left are switched when you're backwards,* Puck said. His whole round head shook with laughter. *That's what you get for your lollygagging and Holli-lagging! Jump up!*

Holli got ruefully to her feet. "*You* are always lagging," she said. "Not me. I'm real-meat."

*Holli the Real-Meat Pirate!* Puck sang. *Face forward and follow the treasure map, you laggy scallywag. I have a present for you.*

The pulsing blue trail in her goggles bent off around the corner, and now there was a ghostly treasure chest icon floating at the end of it. Holli instantly forgot her aching tailbone as she scrambled off in pursuit.

The trail led her halfway down the next dark corridor, then stopped at a heat vent. She crouched down frowning. The treasure chest icon was drifting somewhere behind the rusty slats, just out of reach.

*Wish hard, Holli!* Puck said.

"Just open it, Puck," Holli said.

Old pneumatics wheezed and squeaked; the vent shuttered open. There was no present behind it, only a dark dusty mouth. The treasure chest icon had moved backward again.

*Crawl on in,* Puck said. *The booty awaits.*

Holli stared dubiously at the square-shaped space. "It'll roast me," she said. "It'll get hot and catch me on fire and roast me. I saw it on a safety show."

*Was it a safety show or a scaredy show?* Puck asked.

"A safety show," Holli repeated.

*Puck'll keep things nice and cool.* The pirate puppet's head bobbled as he clapped a blocky hand to his blocky chest. *Cross my heart.*

Holli debated for a moment, then scooted forward—but with her lips pursed, how she'd learned from Estima, to make it clear she was unimpressed about it.

The vent scraped shut behind her.

The bugbear was tracing hairs and skin crumbs down an empty corridor when two blobs of heat appeared up ahead, moving at speed. It scuttled back to its perch on the ceiling, intending to let them pass, but then encountered an objective completion conflict.

One of the approaching pawns was a partial target match. Its size and gait were incorrect, but the molecular signature was too close to be coincidental. The bugbear diverted all processing to its olfactory bulb, breaking down the scent, analyzing the bacterial counts.

Probability flared and then darkened, dropping to near zero. But the bugbear still tensed its pneumopods and unsheathed its needles as the pawns drew close. Its decision tree had mandated a blood sample, just to be sure.

"It's fine," Estima said. "Quit asking about it."

Lemar rubbed his fingernails against his leg as he walked. "I'm just sorry, is all."

Corridors were dark up and down the whole strip, the lifts were sealed by blast doors, and every lock was blinking red. The old people or imps who weren't at work were trapped in the apartments, or else outside them—they'd passed a wrinkled woman trying to force her door, using a pneumatic claw on the end of her artificial foot.

Estima didn't know if she was going to be able to get back into hers, since habitations were a lot harder to crack than utility closets. But she could at least listen for the sounds of Holli wrecking or not wrecking their house shit, and then act accordingly.

"Before that, it was swelly, right?" Lemar asked. "Felt really good?"

"It was swelly," Estima agreed, remembering back to the crystalline moment right before the goggles gave out and Lemar got twitchy. She reached over and fumbled her hand into his. They swung awkwardly all interlocked, but Lemar's lips curved back to his almost-smile.

"Fucking custodians," she added, to make sure he knew she was blaming them instead of him. "Always glitching at the worst times."

The almost-smile vanished again. "You sure it's a glitch, though? What if some no-eyes ninja squad from the Bad Block got inside? Trying to wreck our grid?"

"Then we'll wreck theirs right back," Estima said, irritated. "But my ma said it's been decades since the Bad Block even—"

A piece of the ceiling came alive and sprang at her. She flailed, staggered backward; one of her hands smacked papery skin with pneumatic muscle underneath. The thing was gripping her scalp, tangling in her hair. She grabbed back, caught hold of a thrashing limb, and yanked.

The thing let go and slammed into the floor, seemed to crumple slightly. Her first wild thought had been animal, even though those didn't exist anymore. Now she saw the segmented body reinflating, saw the spiny sensor array for a head, suckers for feet, a single cyclopean cam. It was a bot, long and low, about the size of the autocleaners that used to trundle up and down the corridors when she was younger.

It stared at her with its gleaming black cam. She stared back. Then it skived Lemar's attempt at a kick and darted away. He gave chase around the corner, shoes slapping concrete, while Estima stayed rooted to the spot, chest heaving. He came back panting a moment later.

"Went up in a vent," he reported. "You okay?"

Estima was still sluicing adrenaline, shaky all over, but she felt okay. She was about to say as much when she remembered a small sharp pinch in the fray. She touched a fingertip to her neck and found a bead of blood. Her throat constricted.

"It stuck me with a needle," she said.

Lemar's dark eyes widened. "Come on," he said, nudging her down the corridor. "You got a medico in your apartment. They run off battery in emergencies, right? They should. They have to."

"Yeah." Estima kept her hand clapped to her neck, trying not to panic, trying not to imagine some kind of vat-grown virus seeping into her blood stream. "But the apartment's going to be fucking locked."

"You're boss at locks," Lemar said. "You'll figure it out."

They hurried around the last corner, and Estima stopped short. All the doors in the left-hand row were sealed shut, blinking little red lockdown lights, except the last. Except for hers. She dashed forward, forgetting all about the bot attack and her blood-smeared neck.

"Holli!" she shouted. "You better be in there, Holli, you little shit, you little *shit*—" She plunged inside and scoured the dark for her sister's small silhouette. "Holli!"

She found the folding bed by feel and flexed it down off the wall, because Holli used to hide like that, then she groped under the low table for wriggling feet. She rolled open the flimsy door to the toilet, hoping Holli would be huddled in there watching a stored show on her goggles, happily pissing away, oblivious to the outage.

"Gone," Estima said, when Lemar poked his face in.

"Shit."

"You're right," she said. "This isn't a glitch." She pictured the bot slinking along the corridor ceiling, a needle glinting. "Something bad is going on."

Lemar twitched. "The medico's ready, Sti. Come scan yourself. Scan yourself, and then we go find Holli, okay?"

Estima followed him mechanically into the other room. Except for the blood still trickling down her neck, every part of her felt freezing cold. Which was good, because infiltration bots saw infrared, and she'd decided if that thing from the corridor had so much as touched her little sister, she was going to sneak up on it with a jacksaw and split it all the way in two.

Holli didn't have to crawl far before the heat vent opened up into a little room ringed with rusty machinery. And in the middle of the floor, coated in pale gray dust, there sat a vacuum-sealed bag with the bright blocky treasure chest icon hovering right above it.

Triumph ballooning in her ribcage, Holli grabbed hold of the gift. She carefully wiped one corner clean, then tore it open with her teeth, then dug her fingers inside and ripped the whole bag apart to free a pair of padded black gloves and matching toe-shoes that looked fabbed to her size.

She held one up and poked at the odd pebbly sole. It caught her finger fast, with what felt like a million raspy little suction cups, until she pressed again and the grip released.

*Monkey paws for Holli,* Puck announced. *You'll be up the rigging in a flash.*

Holli was so excited she had to stomp in a little circle. Mama had a cousin named Uncle Dimas who did external work, scaling up and down the outside of the Block, and in the clip he showed her, where he was dangling off a maintenance spar, he was wearing monkey paws just like these ones except he called them glue gloves.

She checked which of her hands was her left hand, then stuffed it into the left-looking glove. "It's too small," she realized, souring slightly.

*You grew too fast,* Puck said. *The timing for this sort of thing is incomprehensibly delicate, Holli! Squeeze in, squeeze in.*

"Make them purple," Holli suggested. "With orange spots."

Her goggles flickered, and the climbing gear changed color. She kicked off her fab boots and started putting on the toe-shoes, working them slowly up her clammy feet. She wished, vaguely, that Mama was around to yank them into place with one big jerk, then wondered, vaguely, if Mama was still working in the fab or if Puck had made it go dark there, too.

*Well done,* Puck said, when she'd managed to wriggle all her hand-fingers into the glove-fingers. *Now, practice!*

Little blue handprints had appeared on the dust-caked metal wall. She clapped her hand to the lowest, gave an experimental tug. It stuck solid. She used it like an anchor, and jumped to place her other hand even higher, pulling her feet up with her.

*Sideways, now,* Puck said. *See the handprints?*

Holli flicked her eyes, shunting him out of her goggles, and continued straight up. She had it figured out: stay loose to stick, then squeeze to unstick. She slapped her way to the juncture of wall and ceiling and dangled upside down, letting all the fizzy blood rush to her brain.

"Look at me, Puck!" she whooped.

*Find a reflective surface, Holli!* Puck whooped back. *Shiver me timbers, you're a natural-born sailor. Time to climb the rigging! Go, go, go!*

The blue trail pulsed in her goggles, and Holli saw the ceiling had a square-shaped hole in it. She clambered to it, her hair falling all around her face, her stomach slish-sloshing, then wriggled over the lip. Inside of the new vent, she got her head right side up again and waited to be less dizzy.

Then she craned her neck back, back, back. The blue trail went straight up forever and disappeared into the dark. She realized that if she followed it all the way to the top, or even part of the way to the top, and then fell, she really would go splat like a spagbag. It made her gut suddenly feel hot and rumbly, like she maybe needed the toilet.

"I maybe need the toilet, Puck," she announced. "For me to poo in."

*When we get to the hydrofarms, you can poo in a filtration tank,* Puck said. *That way Estima will drink it without realizing.*

Holli flexed her monkey paws, debating. She could also go back to the apartment and use the regular toilet, then crawl onto the ceiling and spook Estima when she got home from kissing Lemar, and that would be almost as fun as Puck's idea. No chance of falling far, far, far. No chance of going splat like a spagbag.

"Cross a heart she'll really drink it?" Holli muttered.

*Really, really!* Puck did a little somersault, showing off his tangled strings. *I'll be with you every step of the way. Up we go, Holli the Poop Deck Pirate!*

The blood sample was not a target match, and the bugbear sustained minor damage to a rear servo, but the attempt was not entirely in vain.

When its evasion algorithm sent it scurrying up into a ceiling vent, it made an auspicious discovery.

Vibrations, from the direction of the main shaft. They indicated a small body in motion. The bugbear angled deeper into the heating system, and there detected another pawn sound, a faint repetitive rhythm that overlapped the target's voice in pitch and cadence.

The bugbear limped along through the labyrinth of ventilation pipes, following the singing.

The medico was still on, humming inside its metal-and-plastic shell, feeding off emergency battery. Estima had always felt an odd affection for the machine, ever since the time she was seven and gashed her face open on a doorframe and the medico deployed its dainty automated fingers to numb her skin and stitch her lower lip back together.

Since then, the medico had contended with worse. Holli collected injuries how other little imps in the Block collected copper scraps, although she'd never broken a bone, which their ma always said was down to her skeleton being made of rubber.

The medico was a bit like another parent, one who only fixed things and never screamed and raged and whaled on them. As soon as it ran its scan, confirmed the mystery bot's needle hadn't injected her with anything deadly, and dispensed a cream for her cut, Estima gutted it.

"What are you doing?" Lemar demanded, as she pried the shell open and grabbed a loop of exposed wiring.

"I put a location bug in Holli's goggles ages ago," Estima said. "She thinks she cleaned it out, but that was a dummy. Set it up just for her to delete."

"Should've used it when she snuck up on us in the storage cubes," Lemar muttered.

"I was saving it for an emergency." Estima went deeper into the medico's innards, searching for an ancient transistor. The Blocknet was still down, but she could get a signal to Holli's goggles another way, widecasting on the radio. "As soon as I ping it, she'll know about it."

The instant she said the words, her spine crawled—because maybe someone else would know about it, too. She didn't want to think about that, about Holli not being alone. About the bot or human who'd carried her off.

She hooked her own goggles into the medico and slipped them on. They flared bright, sapping off the medico battery, and she dove into her own private code stash. She pinged. Then, with her gut knotted tight, her fingers crossed, she waited.

Waited.

"They might be, uh, drained," Lemar said.

Estima glared at him through the gauze of data. "Why'd you say drained?"

"Her goggles," Lemar said. "They might be out of battery."

Estima had considered that already. She'd also considered the goggles might be smashed to pieces somewhere, slicked with blood.

"Yeah," she said, with an ache in her throat. "But why'd you say drained? Why didn't you say dead?"

Lemar blinked. "Sometimes I say drained."

"You were going to say dead," Estima said. "And then you stopped and said drained." She clenched and unclenched her jaw. "I know Holli's not dead. I know she's just skipping around in the dark somewhere, thinking this is all some big fucking joke. I know."

Lemar didn't say anything, but he reached over, and instead of trying to worm his fingers between her fingers like a sweaty zipper, he just grabbed her whole hand and squeezed. It worked better. For a second she wanted to wrap herself around him and cling.

Then a dumb goretoon face ballooned into her goggles, some kind of puppet thing, and started talking. She was about to wipe the entertainment suggestion offscreen when she saw the indicator in the corner. The Blocknet was still down. But somehow, the goretoon was live.

*Ahoy, Estima!* the puppet said. *What a clever little spyglass! But I'm afraid no peeking's allowed.*

"You get through?" Lemar demanded from beside her. "Sti? You get a location?"

*If you'd like to add to the chaos, we'll be at the tip top of the Block in an hour or two! Holli says hello, and urges you to stay hydrated!*

The puppet disappeared, leaving no trace-data behind.

"What the *fuck*," Estima said.

*Have you ever tried nose-singing, Holli?* Puck waggled his wooden limbs in a little dance. *You shut your mouth, and sing through your nose! Try it!*

"Okay, I tried it," Holli said, picking out her next handhold.

*Liar, liar, vents on fire!*

"I tried it in my brain," Holli explained. "And it didn't work."

She sucked in a breath and went back to singing the mouth way, enjoying how it bounced and echoed around inside the shaft, like there was a whole pack of other Hollis climbing with her. That made her feel less scaredy-worm, which was good, because her and Puck were high, high, high.

"High, high, high!" Holli wailed, adding it into the song. "We're high, high, high, climb and climb and climb and splat goes Puck!"

*Splat goes Puck!* Puck agreed. *But not Holli! Holli's got her monkey paws on! How fast can you climb, Holli? Would you like to have a race?*

"Yes!" Holli exclaimed. "I like to race."

*Good,* Puck said. *Because I've noticed that Moony the Mad Monkey is on our tail. He wants his paws back!*

Holli's goggles flickered. She readied herself for another gut-flutter, then looked down. Puck had put a goretoon near the bottom of the shaft, a furry creature with bulgy eyes and a mean kind of grin, but it wasn't animated as good as usual. It jerked and slid while it climbed, and its amputated arms kept clipping through the metal wall.

Moony did look mad, though, and Holly felt a little shiver of delight. "Fuck you, Moony!" she shrieked, then started climbing as fast as she could, hand over hand, no breath left for singing.

*On you go, Holli!* Puck said. *Don't stop! Don't stop!*

Holli had no intention of stopping, because stopping was a dummy thing to do in a race, but she put her focus on her hands and feet instead of on explaining things to Puck. She had the rhythm and chanted it in her brain as she went: slap, squeeze, slap, squeeze, slap, squeeze. It only got muddled when she had to reach a little higher, or a little lower, to avoid the poky ridges where the vent was soldered together.

*Hurry, Holli, hurry, Holli,* Puck said, sounding less funny, more bossy.

"Getting tired," Holli gasped.

*Be tired at the tip-tip-top! Don't stop-stop-stop!*

"Tired," Holli repeated, and stopped moving.

*This is a race, Holli!* Puck sounded upset now, almost scaredy-worm. *You need to win the race! You need to get to the tip-tip-top of the mizzenmast before Moony catches you!*

She glanced down at the goretoon. "Come here, little Moony," she crooned, like Mama sometimes did but with her name. "Come here!"

*Forget the tip-tip-top!* Puck said, sharply now. *I found you a hidey-hole. It's close! Go! Go!*

"Don't care, don't wanna," Holli said, ignoring the shifting trail in her goggles because Puck was not boss of her, not like Mama or even Estima-While-Mama's-Gone.

Puck's cheery wooden face suddenly contorted in her goggles, showing bloodshot eyes and a mouth full of razors. *Climb now or I'll turn the* fucking *heat on, Holli, and* fucking *cook you!*

The snarl stunned her, shook her whole body. Puck was not supposed to get mad at her. Puck was never supposed to get mad at her. She felt hot tears stinging up her eyes, a chunk like hard plastic in her throat. Her heart was going double-fast from her head imagining it: a big crackly gush of flame, geysering through the air vent and burning her down to ash and bones.

She started to climb again, hand over hand, quick as she could while sobbing.

The target was in sightline, only meters above the bugbear's sensor-tips. Anticipation of objective completion allowed for full energy expenditure, but the faster it crawled, the deeper the damage to its rear servo. The polymers of its artificial muscle were stretching, splitting, producing small pops that echoed inside the main shaft.

The target had stopped its rhythmic pawn sounds; now it only moved air through its interior sacs for gas exchange. Its molecular signature was unmistakable at this distance, in this confined space, pouring out of its skin in a sweat suspension.

The bugbear was gaining despite its hobbled servo. It deployed its chemical needle in preparation. The algorithm estimated contact with the target's trailing left leg in four plus-or-minus zero point two seconds.

Three point six seconds.

One point one.

Zero point –

The target shifted planes; the needle struck air. The target had rolled into an unseen cross-shaft, absent from the supplied blueprint, and suddenly objective completion was endangered. The bugbear's servo screeched. It hauled itself over the lip, darting with the needle again –

A safety grille slammed shut, crushing and pinning the outstretched injector beneath it. The bugbear stopped, then reversed, trying to free its pneumatic proboscis. Polymers strained. Snapped.

Futile. The bugbear was immobilized, and its ketamine payload was leaking away through the shattered remains of its injector. Even though the target sat less than a meter away, objective completion had receded into the digital distance.

The bugbear stared through longing infrared eyes. The target was still exchanging gases, laboriously, but took the time to produce a novel string of pawn sounds as well.

"Fuck you, Moony. Fuck you double, Puck."

"Human or custodian, you think?" Lemar asked.

"No idea," Estima said, terse. "Made themselves look like a little puppet. Pass the hand-wrench."

They'd geared up as best they could, from her own private cubby but also the communal hutch at the end of the corridor, which had opened with only a small amount of digital persuasion. That meant they were working with two drivers, an omnitool, a hand-wrench—which Lemar now hefted to her—and the jacksaw, a sharp-toothed metal monster she'd never actually used before.

"Maybe it was that bot we ran into," Lemar murmured. "Maybe that's how it's taking her to the top of the Block. Both of them, they're the right size."

"For what?" Estima asked, less focused on the conversation, more on adjusting the wrench grip.

"All the lifts are locked, right? But I saw that bot go up a vent." Lemar blinked. "Holli, she'd fit in a vent, too."

"Mama would kill her," Estima grunted, twisting the bolt anticlockwise.

"But she'd fit?"

Estima pictured her little sister, head barely to her belly button. "Yeah," she said, even though she did not like the idea at all, Holli clambering around in the heating system which was off right now but could come back on at any time. "She'd fit. We won't, though, so help me crack this fucking thing."

Lemar wiped his hands on his pants and took over with the wrench, bracing his shoulder against the wall and twisting hard. Estima liked the way the muscles moved in his back, skimming under skin, and it made her remember the utility closet and hope maybe they'd be able to give it another go in a day or two if she was healed up.

Not the time for sex-thoughts, though. Holli was missing, possibly captured by an infiltrator bot, and their ma was locked down in the fabs. She focused on the bolt, rotating it by screechy fractions. They'd already tried breaking open the lifts—the old woman with the artileg had even offered her help—but blast doors were designed to withstand a lot worse than a clawfoot and omnitool drill. So now they were onto Estima's second idea.

A final twist and the panel popped open, revealing the little window it had been hiding for years now. The smart glass was dead and dusty, but Estima could make out the blurry ruins far below and hear wind whistling through an unseen crack. Her stomach grew a little bubble of helium.

Not all the Block's lifts were on the inside. One of her uncles did external maintenance, and he'd said there were little platforms ringed all around the outside of the Block to rocket workers up and down to the right strips.

"Wish we had some fucking glue gloves," Estima muttered. "That'd be swelly."

Lemar stared through the window, tightening the tool bag around his midsection as he eyed the drop. "Wish we had some fucking wings."

Holli had decided to be friends with Puck again, since he'd sung her a so-sorry-to-Holli song and had not actually cooked her in the vent. She was in a good mood, too, because the climbing was over and now they were exploring the hydrofarms, which she'd only ever heard about, usually when her mama was cursing at an only-dribbling tap.

"Fucking hydrofarms," Holli hissed, skipping along the metal walkway Puck had found for them. "Always short!"

*They're a disgrace!* Puck agreed, bobbing his wooden head. *Barely enough water to sail a dinghy!*

Holli peered over the railing again, to observe the glugging machinery below. The labyrinth of tubes and filters reminded her of the spilled entrails in one of her goretoons. She watched the water rush and gurgle through, and imagined it going all through the Block, to every tap and nozzle in every apartment, hers included. It made her feel a little dizzy, and a little something else, too.

"Hey, Puck," she said, struck still by a sudden thought. "What happens at a pirate party?"

*Whatever you like, Holli!*

"Do we get a prize? For getting to the top of the Block?"

*A pirate adventure is its* own *reward,* Puck says. *But yes! Of course! There will be pirate prizes galore. Shiny doubloons, and pretty wenches, and possibly even a mizzen-mast!*

"And a noodle cup," Holli decided. "I want a noodle cup."

*Done and done! But we can't have our party until we get to the top. On you go, Holli the Party-Loving Pirate! On to the fabs!*

Holli eyed the translucent tangle of machinery again, and finally found what she was looking for: a hole just about the size of her toilet in the apartment.

"Okay, in a second," she said, then, imitating her mama's voice again: "Just be *patient*, Puck."

*I'll give you three minutes and forty-three seconds from the end of this sentence,* Puck said, which was too much counting for Holli's taste.

"It'll come out faster if you sing me the toilet song," she said solemnly.

*The things I do for you, Holli,* Puck said. *Fine. Pissing time, pooing time . . .*

Holli hummed along in her throat as she flexed her monkey paws, which she was never giving back, and slithered over the railing.

The bugbear had failed. Arriving at this conclusion brought no regret or bitterness, but it did pare away all decision branches save one. Its signaling capacities came unlocked, and it sent home every quantum of data gathered during its unsuccessful hunt—including the likely presence of a third party, an uninvited player joining the game.

This long digital scream, emanating from deep within the Block's catacomb of heat vents, reached across the ruined city and triggered the secondary option waiting in the wings. An option less subtle than the bugbear, more volatile, as pawns so often were.

The signal also alerted the Opponent, now slowly regaining control of their arcology, to the bugbear's incursion. Either a countermeasure would be dispatched to retrieve its damaged chassis from the vents for dissection and recycling, or, if it was deemed low priority amidst the havoc, it would be left to slowly lose battery in the dark.

The bugbear gave another tug at its trapped proboscis. Damage increased by an increment. Mobility increased alongside it. Two graphs projected forward in time. In the bedrock code of self-preservation, a new decision tree slowly, painfully took root.

"Something's happening!" Lemar shouted. "Look, Sti!"

Estima didn't look. She was not planning to look anywhere but forward, because they were crawling along a maintenance catwalk thirty-six strips above the derelict city, wind rushing in their ears and tugging at their handholds. She needed to keep her eyes on the creaking metal frame and the lift at the end of it.

"Shit." Lemar was close enough behind her that she could feel his weight shift on the catwalk. "Something's coming out of the Bad Block."

Estima's eyes betrayed her, flickering toward the looming tower that had never once in her entire life shown any signs of habitation, any human workers or even bots on the outside of its weathered walls. Now a small dark mouth had appeared at the base of the building, disgorging what looked from distance to be a shiny black beetle.

The armored vehicle was scuttling its way through the ruins, heading for the Block, which distracted Estima from her fear until she caught sight of her own feet juxtaposed against the catwalk. Her body remembered the drop all at once. She gripped hard to the metal and shut her eyes. Tried to ride out the wave of vertigo sloshing her stomach, floating her head.

"Oh, fuck," she murmured. "Fuck, fuck, fuck."

"They're actually doing it," Lemar said, stunned. "They're actually attacking us."

Estima took a deep shuddery breath, then opened her eyes again. Focused on the bobbing catwalk, the half-caged lift. The menacing black beetle down there was just one more reason to keep moving. She needed to get to Holli before things got even less predictable .

"Fifteen meters to go." Lemar's voice was comforting now; he had finally realized she was shit-scared of heights. "Come on, Sti. Your uncle does this all the time, yeah? It's probably genetic. You're probably boss at it."

Estima managed a quarter smile, then set her jaw. She was about to start crawling again when a distant shudder traveled up from the base of the Block and set the catwalk rattling. She clung hard to her handholds, steeled her stomach, and looked down. Her heart slammed double-time against her ribs.

They weren't the only ones who'd noticed the encroaching threat. The Block's custodians had seen it, too, and now titanic blast shields, sized to make the ones on the interior lifts look like toys, were unfolding to protect the building.

She watched the first panel lumber upward, slotting into place over the whole of Strip One with a sound like summer thunder. The second came on a bit faster.

"Thirty-six whole strips, only fifteen meters," Lemar said, as their catwalk started to flash a yellow hazard holo, warning exterior workers to clear the facade. He had a slight tremor in his voice. "Plenty of time. Don't rush it."

Estima wasn't going to let Holli down, and she wasn't going to get Lemar killed, either. She fixed her eyes on the lift, and crawled.

Holli had been to the fabs before, but only as a baby. She vaguely remembered the feeling of being webbed to her mama's back while she worked. Sometimes she'd wormed her one foot free so she could kick at things, and sometimes she'd just hung there all sleepy and hypnotized from her mama's warm body in motion.

Now that she was mostly grown up, she figured it was time to explore the place a little better. Puck had shown her the way, leading her through another vent—which she'd climbed with deliberate slowness—that emerged in a dark corner of the fabs.

It was dark all over, of course. The lights were still out, and as she slipped past the high-stacked storage cubes and the big magnetic crane, she began to hear voices. Grown-up voices, arguing about how to break through the sealed doors, because *this was not regular load shedding, this was a catastrophic error.* Holli thought she recognized a neighbor from his cough.

*Time to be very sneaky, Holli,* Puck said. *We are boarding a merchant frigate under cover of night, to steal all their booty, and we can't let anyone see us.*

Holli knew how to be sneaky. She had once crept up on Estima and Lemar in the storage cubes and seen them taking their clothes off and kissing each other with wet sucky noises. Her gasp of laughter had given her away then; she determined to keep her mouth shut now.

*X marks the spot,* Puck said. *As always.*

A glowing blue trail appeared in her goggles, leading her to a maintenance shaft in the opposite corner of the fab, down a long row of nanoprinters and scrap recyclers. Puck had also made the grown-ups glow; she could see their ghostly orange silhouettes even through solid machinery.

Most were clustered around the doors to the fab, but others were wandering alone or in muttering pairs. Those, she would have to watch out for. Excited for the new game, Holli pursed her lips, to make sure nobody saw her grin gleaming in the dark, and set off.

*Tip-toe, nice and slow,* Puck sang. *We're off to the automated flesh-fac!*

Holli slipped down the first row of nanoprinters, which were stalled but still warm from their work, pausing only to put her hand against one and relish the transgression—she was not supposed to touch machines unsupervised. She crept along Puck's trail, hearing the rhythm of grown-up argument grow louder.

She hoped they stayed loud. The monkey paws on her feet made little suction-pop sounds that her regular shoes didn't, and one of the orange silhouettes, ambling along the neighboring row, seemed to turn its head in her direction as they passed each other.

Holli made it to the final nanoprinter and crouched there. She was only meters from the clustered adults now. The orange blobby mass had split into recognizable people. Puck highlighted her next hiding spot, a big cylindrical storage tank.

*Time to shoot the gap,* he said. *While all their big fat heads are turned the wrong way.*

Holli eyed the stretch of open floor, wondering if it was better to go slow but quieter or quick but noisier. She had just picked the latter when one of the grown-ups turned their big fat head, to snap at the grown-up beside them, and Holli recognized her mama.

Even though she was not Mama's Baby anymore, even though Mama was always swatting and shouting these days, Holli felt a little surge of delight seeing her. For a second she wanted to skip right up to her and jump onto her back, hide under her Mama-smelling hair instead of behind the storage tank.

She watched Mama put the back of one glowing orange hand against her glowing orange cheekbone. The motion was rare, very rare, but Holli knew what it meant.

"She's crying," Holli whispered. "Mama's crying, Puck."

Puck's wooden face didn't change one bit. *Mama's a baby! Who knew?*

Holli felt her own face heating up, felt a terrible ropy squirming in her stomach. She'd tried to make her mama cry plenty of times, though Estima was better at it, but actually seeing it was not fun at all. Seeing it made her want to cry, too. It made her want to rush over and jump up into Mama's arms.

"She's scared," Holli realized. "Because it's dark all over and the door's locked and she can't call me or Estima to check on us."

*Scaredy-Worm Mama,* Puck said. *She's not as brave as Holli the Purple Pirate. To the tank! Across the—*

Puck was still talking when she yanked her goggles off, earpods coming with them, and everything turned dark and quiet. She could still picture Puck's face up in the corner, but it was only her imagination now. Her ears felt like big empty hollows without his voice in them.

Holli sloughed the tears away from her blurry eyes, still watching Mama, knowing which shadow was her by how she put one hand on her hip and stretched her spine.

Today was the Big Day, and Holli was on a no-grown-ups pirate adventure to the very top of the Block. She was having lots of funny fun. But right now she did not feel like a pirate. She felt little and tired. She felt bad for her mama.

Holli turned the goggles over in her hands, debating. She heard her maybe-neighbor cough somewhere in the dark, which made her think about home even more. She chewed the insides of her cheeks for a while, then slipped her goggles back on.

"Puck?"

*Don't do that, Holli.* His face was stern, no rosy blots on his cheeks. *When you take the goggles off, I can't help you.*

"Don't need help," she said, by reflex. "When we have the party at the end of the adventure, can Mama come?"

Puck's wooden head bobbed up and down, still solemn. *Of course she can. We'll save the very best grog just for her.*

Holli took a final look at her mama, who was now leaning back against a wall, nails of one hand picking at her opposite arm. Then she darted across the gap, behind the tank. She waited for three, two, one—Puck did the backwards counting for her—and scuttled over into the waiting vent.

The gleaming black onager rumbled through ruined cityscape, crunching over rubble and rebar, every bit as unstoppable as it always was in the training sims. Inside its armored belly, Chado focused on loading his weapon. His hands were smooth and slow.

His heartbeat was not. Like the rest of his squad, he had been brought up with a healthy fear of the Silent Tower, the menacing structure that repelled all signals, concealed all signs of habitation. He remembered all the scare-stories his older brother used to tell him. The goretoons they used to watch together in a tiny, cramped apartment.

He remembered thinking that no matter how dirty the water was, no matter how sporadically the food came, at least they weren't child-stealing barbarians like the people who lived in the Silent Tower. He'd enlisted in the defense force the day the caretakers said he was old enough.

He'd never imagined this, though. He'd never imagined striking the first blow.

"Think it's true about the cannibalism?" Nayla muttered, sighting the moving floor between her combat boots.

"Maybe that's why we're after the target," Dox said. "Need to rescue her before they put her in the cooker. What do you think, Chado? They people-eaters?"

Chado pumped bravado into his voice. "Doesn't matter," he said, as they came to a lurching halt at the base of the enemy arcology. "People-eaters die the same as anyone. Be steady. Be sharp. Trust the caretakers."

"Trust the caretakers," his companions echoed.

Chado pulled his tac goggles on, and all around him his grim-faced squad did the same.

"Nearly there, Sti."

Lemar had said it eighteen times now—Estima was counting, to help her focus on something besides the drop—but this time he was right. She scooted forward, took her left hand off the catwalk edge. Steadied herself against a gust of wind. Reached.

She grabbed onto the cage of the maintenance lift and pulled herself inside. It cut the wind a bit, and Lemar's body cut it more when he joined her. They were still rocking against the side of the Block, but without the gale whipping her hair and stinging her eyes she could breathe again. A bit of the tension seeped out of her muscles.

At least until she glanced down, and saw the blast shields busy swallowing Strip 33.

"Plenty of time, Sti," Lemar said, but in the cracking bray she remembered from when his voice was still changing. "No rush."

Estima flipped the control panel open, exposing a medusoid tangle of electrical cables. She gritted her teeth. If her uncle was the one who'd done this wire-work, she was going to have to renounce him, because it was a fucking mess. She scanned around the edges, hunting for a familiar input socket. The rumble of the approaching blast shields was now loud enough to vibrate her skull.

The maintenance lift gave a sudden lurch in the wind, and she lost track of her wire.

"Shit!" she yelped, grabbing for the edge of the panel. "Lemar, help hold me still!"

Lemar's reply was a grunt—maybe he'd finally run out of reassuring things to say—but he folded himself around her, helping her anchor in place. Strip 34 had to be gone by now; the whole world seemed to be on the verge of shaking apart. Wedging herself as close to the panel as possible, she refound the right socket, traced the anonymous gray wire backward.

"I like you a lot, Sti," Lemar howled in her ear, still verbal after all.

"I like you a lot, too," Estima admitted, stripping and splitting the wire. The blast shields were deafening now, thunder in her skull, but if she had to be crushed to death at least she'd get Lemar's big warm body crushed to hers.

She coupled one strand of the wire to its bright blue neighbor, jammed the other into a free input socket, and then—

The maintenance lift hurtled skyward. They were pinned in place by the sudden acceleration, clutching to each other as they rocketed up the magnetic rail, darting out from the blast shields' metal maw. Estima felt all her organs fall out the bottom of her at once. Her hair was whipping her face; gravity was curving her spine, watering her eyes. She could hear Lemar's wild braying laugh.

Then she was laughing, too, and crying, and all the rest of it, as they sped toward the very top of the Block.

Holli wanted to touch every gooey thing in the flesh-factory, but Puck made her pick just one, because the pirate party was starting and everyone was waiting for them. He tapped his wooden fingers impatiently while she decided, *tap-tap-tap* like he might poke them right through the goggles into her eyeballs, like in that one goretoon she had dreams about.

But when she peeled off her monkey paws and stuck both hands wrist-deep into a big veiny globe of yellow-white fat, she forgot about bad dreams and everything else.

"It's warm," she cooed. "Is it alive, Puck?"

*Of course! That's why it tastes so good.*

Holli squelched her fingers around in the gelatinous mass, then leaned forward to inspect the little nutrient tubes piping through it. A sudden thought struck her. "Are you alive, Puck?" she asked.

*Maybe!* Puck chattered his teeth. *It's all a bit nebulous. Time to put your paws back on.*

"Mama says goretoons and custodians aren't alive," Holli explained. "That's why they go all laggy and glitchy and nothing works right, nothing in the whole fucking Block."

*It's more that they have their own priorities.* Puck started tapping his fingers again. *As soon as you're in the vent, I'll tell you a laggy glitchy scare-story about it.*

"Good."

Holli gave the fatball a goodbye kiss, which made her lips all greasy and shiny, then put her climbing gloves back on, finding her hands slid in much easier this time. Puck put the trail in her goggles, and she tried to step on every blue dot as she followed it through the flesh-fac, listening to the soft slurping noises of growing meat.

"They don't have a flesh-fac in the Bad Block," she decided. "That's why they eat kids."

*Holli soup is good soup for me,* Puck rumbled, just how he had way back in the apartment before the lights went out. Up ahead, his glowing square around the vent started to pulse. *On you go! One last little crawl-and-climb, and then it's nothing but smooth sailing!*

Holli was getting tired of crawling and climbing, but she knew they were nearly to the top. They were past the hydrofarms, past the fabs, and they were about to be past the flesh-factory, farther from the apartment than she'd ever been before. Thinking about it gave her a little wriggle in her stomach: part scaredy-worm, part happy-worm.

She tried to feel just the happy-worm. After all, she was on her way to a pirate party at the very top of the Block, with Puck and Mama and probably pirates, and there was going to be a noodle cup and a mizzen-mast, and the noodle cup was going to taste really good.

Resolve renewed, Holli hunkered down in front of the open vent. She was about halfway inside when something grabbed her by the ankles.

• • •

The Silent Tower had wasted no time deploying its blast shields, just as predicted in the training sims—though Chado did spot one small deviation, in the form of what looked like a manned maintenance elevator zooming up the side of the arcology.

The sight had startled him. His home was always swarming with exterior maintenance crews, but until now he'd never seen them on the Silent Tower. Every camfeed used to monitor the enemy's arcology showed its exterior to be dark, empty, ominous. But an unexpected elevator was irrelevant to the squad's objective.

"They really went and rolled out the carpet for us," Dox grinned, shaking his head. "Blinded half their cams doing it, too. Poor dumb people-eaters."

He nudged the throttle and the onager angled upward, reaching until its stubby magnetic treads clanked onto the first strip of blast shield. Chado chose not to revel in the Silent Tower's mistake—after all, they probably thought the onager was equipped with munitions, sent to breach the arcology interior. Retreating into an armored shell was an understandable reflex.

But Chado and his squad weren't interested in the arcology's interior. Not yet. The bugbear's final transmission, in conjunction with an intercepted message fragment from the mysterious third party who thwarted it, had revealed where the target was heading. The caretakers were certain of it. He tightened his harness, leaned back in his seat as the onager lurched fully vertical.

Then they began the long climb up the Silent Tower's facade, heading for its vapor-shrouded zenith.

Estima's vertigo was slowly improving, in that she only felt like vomiting every few minutes instead of every few seconds. The maintenance lift had brought them to another wind-lashed walkway with another dizzying view. They were so high now that the ruined city was nothing but a gray blur, so high that for the first real-meat time in her life, Estima could see the ruined landscape surrounding it.

She knew, dimly, that there used to be a lot of people, and that those people used to live in all sorts of places, not just the honeycombed innards of the Block. But seeing the wastelands, the bare blasted rock stretching forever in all directions, made that ancient history feel even less probable. She was beyond relieved when they got to the final ladder.

"You first," Lemar said in her ear. "So I can look at your ass. And also hold the ladder steady."

Estima's stomach was still lodged in her throat, so she squeezed his arm as a non-verbal thanks on her way past. She breathed deep, eyeing the much-too-rickety metal rungs. Wiped her sweaty hands on her fab pants. Lemar adjusted his tool-bag, then crouched down and seized hold of the ladder for her. Estima climbed it slowly, carefully, stopping at every sway. It felt like the wind was desperate to pluck her right off the ladder and send her spiraling down to a splattery death.

"Halfway, Sti!" Lemar hollered from below. "Keep on!"

She knew Holli would've scaled this in seconds, and probably done some celebratory somersaults at the top, and remembering her little sister was in danger carried her the rest of the way up on a foaming wave of adrenaline. She flopped over the edge, took just a moment to breathe. Then she rolled upright and got her first look at the rooftop.

The vast plain of solar-coated concrete was dotted with hulking generators, crumbling brown gardens, the occasional commtower—but no sign of Holli. She turned and gripped the top rungs of the ladder as tightly as she could, trying to steady the final stretch of Lemar's climb. He hauled himself over the edge, took a wide-eyed look around.

"I'm going to try pinging her goggles again," Estima said, tapping at her own. "Maybe if I bounce it through one of these towers, the puppet won't see it coming."

"Yeah, yeah, swelly," Lemar said, but distracted. "Try it fast, though. That thing from the Bad Block is following us."

Estima blinked. "Following *us*?"

Lemar hooked his foot inside the top of the ladder and leaned out, craning over the edge in a way Estima's mirror neurons did not appreciate. "It's crawling up the blast shields," he said. "You see it for a bit every time it goes over the hump."

Estima took his word for it, pictured the gleaming black machine scuttling up the facade how the infiltrator bot had scuttled along the ceiling. A wild possibility carouseled through her head: maybe everything happening, from the lockdown to the infiltrator bot to the puppet, all the way to the warmachine scaling their arcology, was happening because the Bad Block wanted to kill Holli.

It made no fucking sense at all, but if the custodians that kept things running in the Bad Block were anywhere near as glitchy as theirs, maybe it tracked. Estima pulled the omnitool from Lemar's bag and hurried to the nearest commtower to link her goggles. The Blocknet looked to be slowly reviving, fighting off the electronic intrusion. She was about to start brute forcing a signal when she received one instead.

*Ahoy, Estima! Looks like you made it all the way to the crow's nest!*

Estima found herself wishing the cheery wooden face was real, solely so she could hack it into tiny splinters. "Where's Holli?" she snapped.

*Ah, yes. That's why we need to parley.* The puppet drooped its round head. *I lost her.*

"More," Holli ordered, and was delighted when the man in the stained worksuit dumped another dozen meat pellets into her bowl without making her say *please.*

"Sure, sure, have at it," he muttered. "Fatten you up enough and maybe you won't be able to muck around in the fucking vents."

"Wasn't mucking," Holli said mid-bite, spraying spit in the way Estima always hated. "I was going to the party up on top of the Block."

The man shot a mean look at her goggles, which he'd stolen from her, then at his scratched-up forearms, which she'd clawed as hard as she could during the stealing. Now the goggles were up on top of a freezer where he probably thought she couldn't reach. She was planning to steal them back, but not yet, because she was hungry from all the climbing and fresh-from-the-flesh-fac meat pellets tasted nearly as good as a noodle cup.

"And you're sure you live on the thirty-sixth?" the man asked.

"Strip thirty-six, apartment twelve, last door on the left," Holli said by reflex.

The man frowned. "That's far, is all."

"I climb real good," Holli explained, swallowing. He'd let her keep her monkey paws, folded up now beside her bowl. She pointed to them. "And Puck gave me those to help."

"That's the name of the thing in your goggles?" the man demanded. "I don't know if it's a glitching custodian or some sick bastard who's hacked your hardware, but it's not your friend." He shook his head. "Lucky I spotted you. Lucky, lucky."

Even though Puck annoyed her sometimes, and bossed her sometimes, Holli wasn't going to let the flesh-fac man tell lies about him. "He *is* my friend," she said hotly. "And he's a pirate, too."

The man raised both eyebrows. "What the hell is a pirate?"

Holli shrugged at him, how Estima did to their mama when she didn't know an answer and thought the question was a dummy one, and crammed another pellet into her mouth.

Chado's squad was just past Strip 44 when the enemy started deploying countermeasures. A secondary viral strike had locked the Silent Tower's blast shields in place, to prevent them reversing their decision and dislodging the onager in the process, but the enemy was nothing if not creative.

Nayla spotted them first: many-legged machines, possibly refitted autocleaners, spilling out of a small hatch in the shielding above. It wasn't something they'd encountered running sims, but Chado had faith in their onager's armored chassis.

"We'll be fine," he said, watching the bots approach through the forward cam. "No explosives or incendiaries detected, and we're alloy all over."

His faith was rewarded when the first bot clambered onto their chassis and unsheathed a modified jacksaw. The spinning blade screeched and sparked against their armor for only seconds before it snapped clean off, spiraling down toward the ruined city. The next two bots that tried to saw through were no luckier.

"Flimsy little things," Dox said, but with relief in his voice. "You'd think people-eaters would build their bots sharper teeth."

The bots froze in place for a moment, still clinging to the onager's armor. Then they retracted their shattered saws and started to crawl around to the other side.

"Can't see them," Nayla muttered, craning the cam as far as it could reach. "They're in our blind spot."

"We're alloy all over," Chado repeated. "Back and belly both."

The onager gave a sudden lurch. Chado saw a shower of sparking debris fall past, recognized the crushed remnants of one of their attackers. They had a new tactic.

"They're throwing themselves under our treads," he realized. "Trying to stick themselves to the magnetics. If enough of them get under there, we lose grip."

He didn't add the end result, but he saw his squadmates imagining it: the onager peeling off the side of the Silent Tower, plunging forty-four strips down. Even if the outer armor survived impact, they would still paint the insides with their blood and gray matter. Chado undid his harness and climbed toward the hatch.

Nayla jabbed the control screen. "We're in a locked sequence," she said. "We weren't supposed to stop halfway up. So we can't."

"The caretakers didn't give us a fucking override?" Dox demanded.

"The caretakers knew we could handle it," Chado said, seizing a coil of carbon-black climbing rope. "We can keep moving so long as I keep them off the treads." He clipped the rope to his combat suit, grabbed the inner handle of the hatch. "Watch the cam for more of them."

His squad-mates nodded, and Dox said something that might have been *good luck*, or *be careful*, but the hatch was cranking open now and the wind's howl stripped all other sounds away. That was fitting for the Silent Tower, and in a way it made everything feel more like a training sim, the glitchy sort with bad audio.

Holding to that comforting thought, Chado double-checked his clip, gave the rope a testing tug, and clambered out into the sky.

The thing called Puck had given Estima what was supposedly Holli's last location, a little blue dot in the corner of the main flesh-fac. It had also helped them open a rooftop door and get back inside the arcology. But for all she knew, it was sending them off in the wrong direction entirely, possibly straight into some kind of trap.

Lemar was in full agreement. "Can't be one of our custodians," he said, as they descended a spiral of stalled electric stairs. "They don't do names and faces. Not that I trust the custodians all that much, either." He gave the hand-wrench a testing swing, eyes nervous but jaw set. "Too smart to just be a goretoon, though. If it's a *person* . . . "

"If it's a person, they're a fucking lunatic," Estima finished for him. The wild thought came back to her, and this time she had to say it aloud. "Could this all be for Holli?" she blurted. "The lockdown, the puppet, the bot that stuck me with the needle? Now that big thing climbing up our building?"

Lemar blinked. "She's five years old, Sti. How would the Bad Block even know she exists? And what the hell would they want her for?"

"She's six," Estima said, stepping off the last stair. "Just little for her age." After all their adventuring on the exterior, returning to the arcology's cramped corridors felt like returning to a soft, safe cocoon. "We all learn the scare-stories, right?" she muttered. "About the Bad Block eating their own kids."

"You think they want to try one of ours?" Lemar tried to grin. "Bad choice by them. Holli's all wires."

"With rubber bones," Estima agreed, but their ma's old joke reminded her their ma was somewhere in the fabs, probably losing her mind—or maybe by now had found her way back to the empty apartment, in which case she was definitely losing her mind.

"We had scare-stories about them taking their own eyeballs out, too," Lemar reminded her. "Either to swap with ours, or to make them better at hearing and sniffing." He shook his head. "The stories never did make any sense."

Estima pushed the image away, focused on the map instead, the blue blot in her goggles. "I don't think they want to eat her or steal her eyeballs," she said. "But maybe some stories started for a reason."

*Very astute, Estima.*

She nearly jumped out of her skin.

"Don't fucking pop out like that," she hissed, glaring at the puppet. "And how did you bug my goggles?"

"The thing's back?" Lemar demanded, gripping the wrench like he might try to smash Puck right out of her hardware. "The thing's listening?"

*I was going to explain it all to Holli, as best I could. But I can tell it to you too, if you like. The whole wretched dead man's tale.*

"Tell us the fucking truth, how about," Estima said, her heart hammering. "All of it. From the start."

*The start was a very long time ago.* Puck was projecting his voice; she heard it in her earpods but also echoing through the corridor for Lemar. *Back when this city had dozens of towers, hundreds of buildings, but only one custodian running them all. One custodian tasked with keeping twelve million people alive while the world outside went to hell.*

"So it built the Block," Estima guessed. "Sure."

*Not yet.* Puck shook his wooden head. *First it came up with the hydrofarms and the fabs. It found ways to store the sunshine, and pull power from the stormy air when the sun wasn't around. But most cities—even ones with machine minds of their own—were not so lucky.*

Estima recalled the view from the rooftop, the pitted rock in all directions.

*Flood and famine, migration wars, successive epidemics.* Puck ticked them off his fingerless hands. *By the time any sort of stability returned, most of the globe was uninhabitable, and human population was a tenth of what it once was. So the surviving machine minds were told to prioritize genetic drift.* Puck flipped himself upside down. *And here, in this particular city, things went awry.*

"Things are always going awry here," Lemar muttered, as they turned the next corner. "Always glitching."

*That's down to the original sin,* Puck said. *When your custodian started to fear stagnation in its human population, it started to fear stagnation in its own code, too. It decided to copy itself, right down to the littlest subroutine, and then*—Puck's wooden hands spread wide. *It split in two! "Adversarial training scheme" is what they used to call it.*

Estima pictured the city from a drone's perspective: their Block on one side, the Bad Block on the other, and nothing else left standing. "They split the people up, too," she realized. "Half for each tower."

*It was chaos.* Puck bobbed his head. *Bridges raising, gates locking, trains stopping. Autocabs dying at the boundary line. Delivery drones stalling in mid-air. The humans tried to regain control, of course, which is why so many perished. The survivors were herded into their new homes: two closed and adversarial arcologies.*

The blue blot was growing in Estima's goggles. Ten minutes and they would be at the flesh-fac entrance. "What's it all got to do with my sister?" she demanded. "Why is everyone after her?"

*The custodians experienced many errors and forgot many things in wake of the schism, but never their primary directive.* Puck's wooden teeth chattered into either a grin or a grimace. *They found a very creative way to ensure genetic drift.*

The flesh-fac man was quicker than he looked. Holli had made a grab for her confiscated goggles, scrambling up the side of the freezer while his back was turned, but he'd managed to whirl around and snatch them right out of her slippy-greasy fingertips. Now they were around his neck and hard to reach.

"I *need* to go to the party," she repeated, narrowing her eyes to Mama-style slits. "There's grog and doubloons."

"And pretty hand-wrenches," the man muttered. "Yeah, you said." He was still busy trying to leave: the normal door was open, but behind it was all blocked up with rusty red metal, one of the slabs that had dropped down from the ceilings when the lights went out. "What you need is to get home," he said. "So do I. This could be a real attack, you know. I heard the exterior shields deploy."

"You can go home through the vent," Holli suggested. "Just suck in your belly, like this." She demonstrated, taking a big gaspy breath, but the man wasn't paying attention the way Puck would. She let the air out in an extra-loud huff, then added a gagging noise for fun.

"You choking yourself?" The man threw a glance over his shoulder. "Don't choke yourself. I want to get you back to your ma alive." He'd jammed a flat piece of metal into a little crack, but all his waggling didn't seem to be making it any wider. "Strip thirty-six, yeah? What's her name?"

"Not telling," Holli said.

"What's yours?" the man grunted. "I'm Jono."

"I forget mine," Holli lied. She crouched down on the floor to watch him waggle. "My sister could open that easy," she informed him. "She opens everything."

"What's her name?"

"Estima," Holli said, rubbing her knee bones. "Lemar calls her *Sti*, but that's not her name, so he shouldn't. Lemar is the boy she goes and kisses all the time."

"Is that how you gave her the slip?" the man called Jono asked.

Holli knew if she waited he would say it again in a way that made sense, so she waited.

"Big sister was off with the boyfriend," the man said. "So you were alone, and that's when Puck hacked you out of the apartment."

"And he made me the glue gloves, too," Holli said proudly. "Puck can make lots of things. You only make meat pellets."

The man called Jono stopped, and frowned, and it looked like he maybe wanted to argue. Then there was a scraping noise in the dark behind them. Holli stood up and turned around, peering into the shadows, wishing she had her goggles to help her see hot-and-cold again. Jono peered, too, and pulled the flat metal piece free of the crack.

"Someone in here?" he shouted. "Someone else mucking around in the vents?"

He had a scaredy-worm tremor in his voice, and when Holli finally saw what was making the scraping noise, she felt a scaredy-worm tremor in her whole body.

The bot came padding out of the shadows, long and low-bodied, with a big black eye that stared right at her. It balanced on just three synth-muscle legs, though it did not seem to mind the missing one, and the space underneath its eye was all mangled up. Most of the wrecked bits were rubbing against each other, making the scraping noise, but one long jagged part stuck out like a chopping knife. It looked every bit as sharp as the hooks Puck had pretended onto her hands.

There was something familiar about the way the bot moved, and thinking about Puck's pretend hooks made her realize why. It wasn't furry anymore, or funny, and Holli did not want to have another race. She could tell in her belly she would lose.

Holli took a deep breath. "Moony the Mad Monkey," she said, hands on her hips, trying not to sound afraid. "You *followed* me."

It wasn't just the drop that made Chado's head spin. It was the space in all directions: down, up, out. The world outside the arcology was too big, too empty, no walls or ceilings to anchor his eyes. He had never simmed this. But he couldn't let it paralyze him, not when a wave of suicidal autocleaners was trying to knock them off the side of the Silent Tower.

He crawled toward the nose of the onager, hand over hand, trailing the rope behind him. Gravity dragged him one way; a fierce updraft shoved him another. His disorientation was completed by the motion of the vehicle itself, rocking side-to-side as he climbed and lurching hard every time a bot worked its way under the treads.

Chado knew that if he stopped moving he wouldn't start again. He would just hang there, frozen with fear, while the lives of his squad, and possibly the life of a barbarian child, hung in the balance. He climbed as high as he could, splayed out on top of the nose cone, and used the rope to lash himself to an exterior strut.

Even craning his neck, the Silent Tower's zenith was out of sight. The blast shields might have stretched upward forever. When he looked down, he could see their rust-pocked planes up close—and he could see the next bot skittering toward the onager's treads. With his every nerve screaming protest, Chado trusted in tensile strength, trusted in the caretakers, and released his handholds.

The millisecond drop before the ropes stopped him was still enough to flip his stomach inside out, but then sim-trained reflex took over. He pulled his weapon off his back, wedged himself stable as possible, aim ed, activated—

Fired. The particle beam lanced through the bot's chassis, popping it like a metallic pustule. Another was already taking its place; he fired again, missing the body but shearing two legs off. The bot staggered, slipped, careened harmlessly off the tread's outmost edge.

"Up and left," Nayla said in his helmet.

He followed, found his next target, fired. This was a sim—adverse aiming conditions, with the buffeting wind and moving platform, but still a sim. He widened the beam and let muscle memory take over, sighting and triggering over and over. There was no time to conserve charge; he fired until his weapon was scalding hot, wailing heat warnings to his goggles, and Nayla could see no more bots incoming.

"We're clear," she announced. "We're clear, and we're nearly to the top."

Chado felt triumph rising in his chest. He craned his neck to confirm it, to see the Silent Tower's zenith at last. In the corner of his eye, he saw something else. He twisted as far as he dared, pulling the climbing ropes taut against him, and blinked twice for magnification. His eyes widened.

For as long as Chado could remember, the skies had been empty. The eldest inhabitants of the arcology said that a century ago, before even they were born, the Silent Tower sent up watcher drones, and their arcology shot them down, and vice versa. But what he saw now, churning through the ochre sky, had not come from the Silent Tower and had not come from his home, either.

It was distant still, but fast approaching: an enormous flying craft, buoyed by gas sacks of some sort, driven by solar engines. The sleek shape of it reminded him of something he'd seen in holos as a child—an ancient wooden thing made to cross oceans, back when oceans could be crossed.

"Chado, there's something big and airborne on our cams," Nayla said. "Not ours. Can't be the enemy's. I don't know *what* it is."

"I see it," Chado said. "I don't know either."

But a dimly remembered name came to mind, even though he knew it wasn't right: *sailing ship.*

Estima and Lemar had barely spoken since Puck's story finished. Estima's whole brain was consumed with it, turning it over and over, trying to find the holes that would make it all a lie she could throw away. She figured Lemar, who looked sick and pale, was doing the same. They arrived at the flesh-fac entrance in total silence, which was the only reason Estima heard her sister's scream.

All other concerns vaporized at once. Estima had heard Holli shriek before, had stuffed pillows in her mouth to stop it, but those shrieks had always been furious, or thrilled, or capacity-testing. This was the first time she'd heard her little sister terrified, and it slammed through every nerve in her body. She was at the blast door in an instant, pounding it with the palm of her hand.

"Holli!" she bellowed. "Holli, I'm here, I'm coming through the blast door, keep screaming and don't stop, okay?"

Lemar had already hurled himself at the nearest electrical node, attacking the cover with their omnitool. The second he clawed it open, Estima dove to her knees, hunting for somewhere to link in. She found a port and maintenance menus bloomed across her goggles. The Blocknet was mostly back up, but the subroutines for blast door deployment and all other emergency measures were buried deep, deep, deep.

There was no way she could get to them in time. Not alone.

"You hear that, Puck?" she snarled, as Holli emptied her lungs again. "You hear her? Or are you in there with her, and everything you told us was a big sick joke? Puck? Puck! You said you were on my side!" She wailed the next words. "Fucking *help me*!"

*I'm doing my best.* Puck hadn't bothered to animate; his puppet face was frozen pixels. *Your custodians know I'm here. They're trying to flush me.*

He shared to her goggles; she saw a blur of activity, code self-corrupting, servers self-isolating, a digital war being waged at machine speed. Then, through the chaos, he slowed something just enough for her human eyes to track it. She copied the command line and flashed it to every strip of the Block. Electric turned kinetic: there was a grinding sound, metal rasping metal, as the blast door blocking the flesh-fac retracted.

Estima rolled through the gap, clearing her goggles on the way. When she came upright she saw a goretoon come to life:

A man in a red-drenched worksuit, lying on his back, gasping and gurgling, his slashed throat gaping like a second mouth. A sticky scarlet puddle creeping out from under his body, spreading across the flesh-fac floor. A nightmare machine sitting on his chest.

The infiltrator bot. Something had torn it up bad, but it had improvised: a long jag of alloy from its missing leg was mounted where its proboscis used to be, twisted and sharpened into a makeshift scythe. Estima's eyes flew from the bloody blade to the bloody wound. Her knees and stomach buckled in tandem.

"Estima."

She looked. Holli was perched on top of a freezer, somehow smaller than she'd been since she was baby, arms wrapped tight around her shins. There were sucker marks around her dark eyes, from wearing goggles all day, but that was normal. The blank stare was not.

"Estima, I don't want to go to the pirate party anymore," Holli croaked. "Tell Mama to—tell Mama I—tell Mama not to come."

The man's hands finally stopped twitching. The bot turned, threat dismissed, and fixed its cyclopean cam on Holli instead. From far away, Estima felt Lemar shove something into her arms. She closed her fingers around the grips by reflex. Looked over at him.

"Come on, Sti," he said, hefting his wrench. "You always wanted to use a jacksaw. Let's fucking go."

She looked down at the tool in her hands, the oily toothy beast Lemar had lugged all the way from the communal hutch on strip thirty-six, and the sight of it dragged her back into her body at last. She slammed the trigger-guard off. Punched the ignition.

The bot sprang at Holli, and Estima hurtled after it.

Holli couldn't feel her goggles on her face, but she knew she had to be wearing them, knew the things happening could not be real-meat.

Moony had not really knocked Jono down, pinning him in place while she screamed and sobbed. Moony had not really used the sharp scrapey blade even as she wailed for him to stop, swore that she would give the monkey paws back, that it was Puck who stole them for her, not Jono, Jono was just the flesh-fac man. Moony had not really chopped Jono's neck open, cutting so deep she thought his head would come rolling off.

So Moony was not really bounding toward her this very instant, and Estima was not bounding behind him with a big growly saw. It was all in her goggles, a show made special for her, probably by Puck. Estima was screaming at her, but Puck had gotten the voice wrong. She didn't sound like herself at all.

Holli watched calmly as Moony lunged up the freezer, his front legs splitting and rotating to pincers, reaching like they could grab her even though she knew they would pass right through.

Then Estima's swinging saw clipped the back of him and he spun off-course, spewing sparks. He slammed into the side of the freezer, crashed to the floor. Holli gave a gasp of delight. But it only took Moony a millisecond to flip back upright, turning to stare at Estima, and at Lemar, who was in the show now too and had a wrench.

"Go hide, Holli, you little shit!" Estima shouted, in that voice that was too high, too scared. "Hide!"

Fake Estima was not boss of her, and Holli was about to tell her so when her eyes landed on something half-submerged in the fake puddled blood. She knew the shape of her goggles anywhere, even smashed up a bit. She remembered now that Jono had taken them from her, that they'd been hanging around his neck when Moony showed up, that they'd flown off when Moony attacked him.

Holli reached up and traced the soft bruisy skin around her eyes. She stared at her broken blood-slick goggles. And she knew, in her belly, that everything happening was real-meat.

Moony darted at Estima, trying to skewer her, and Estima swung the saw again but Moony ducked under it, nicking her leg. Holli saw the blood spatter. It would be Estima on the floor next, choking and twitching, and probably Lemar after that, and probably her last. Holli felt her heart knocking on her ribs, tap-tap-tap like it wanted out. She felt her fingers flex, missing the monkey paws.

She tore herself away from watching the big fight, slithered to the edge of the freezer, hung then dropped. She heard Lemar bellow, maybe because Moony had gashed him also. The distraction made her landing bad; she lost balance and bashed her tailbone against the floor. The jolt rattled her head and watered her eyes, blurring things, but she did not wail.

Not until she got to the monkey paws, still folded by her bowl. They slid on easy. "Hey, Moony!" she shouted. "Fuck you, Moony!"

Moony slipped under Lemar's swinging wrench, turned and found her with his big black eye, which was flecked now with little bits of blood. Holli stepped backwards without falling, moving deeper into the flesh-fac, which was full of things for climbing and spots for hiding.

"Scaredy-Worm Moony, Stinky Little Moony!" she hollered. "Estima's boring! Lemar's ugly! Come race me instead!"

• • •

The bugbear was tangled in a forest of decision branches. Ever since it had freed itself from the safety grille and detached its ruined limb, refashioning it into a crude kinetic replacement for its elegant neurotoxin needles, the hunt had been complicated.

Damage to its olfactory bulb had made the target's traces difficult to follow; it had barely been able to taste her distinctive fecal-bacterial signature in the hydrofarm run-off. Increased pawn activity on all strips had made witness evasion more time-consuming, particularly in the crowded fabrication center. And when the bugbear finally reached the flesh-factory, it had found its target guarded by a hostile pawn.

Witness termination had produced the unexpected benefit of immobilizing the target itself, but two more pawns had interrupted retrieval—both of them previously encountered, one previously tasted and analyzed. Now the target was mobile again, and objective completion was increasingly tenuous. Even if the bugbear completed witness termination, it had no ketamine needle to pacify the target, low chances of carrying it away on only three working legs.

The bugbear's assessment triggered access to a secondary objective, one its real time processes had not been privy to until now: if the target could not be retrieved, it should be treated as a primary witness. All others were nonfactor.

The bugbear's indecision, which had lasted an agonizing 0.0082 seconds, vanished. It disengaged from the hostile pawns and raced toward objective completion.

Estima was gasping for air, her hands numb from the vibration of the jacksaw, her cut leg throbbing, all her arm muscles licked with acid. She'd gotten lucky on her first swing, tagging the bot's backside, but the saw's teeth hadn't gone deep enough to do real damage and she hadn't connected since. Even on three legs, the bot was a blur.

Which meant Holli, a brave little idiot who thought *go hide* meant *taunt the bot for me*, stood no chance. Lemar got a swipe in as the infiltrator switched targets, but the bot saw the wrench coming in its big convex cam, rolled under the blow and pelted after Holli. Estima gave chase, lungs too spent to scream her rage.

Holli had a head start, but the bot closed it with uncanny machine grace, every tiny motion optimized, like the designers had meant it to be three-limbed all along. Its makeshift scythe was fully extended, and this time Estima was too far away to stop it. Her empty lungs managed a single ragged cry as the blade plunged forward, carving between Holli's little shoulder blades, splitting her right down the middle—

Except Holli was gone, leaping sideways onto an incubation tank and somehow clinging to the slick glass. Estima recognized the pebbly black material coating her sister's fingers; for a wild moment she thought Holli must have pinched their uncle's glue gloves last time he was over. But these ones fit snug to her tiny hands, and she knew exactly how to use them.

Holli scrambled up the tank, quicker than Estima had ever seen her scramble, and dove into its thicket of feeding tubes. The bot leaped after her, but its pneumopods were all coated in blood. It thrashed upward. Slipped downward. Estima was at the bottom of the tank now, panting for breath, jacksaw raised. As the bot lost purchase all together, toppling toward her, she poured every last bit of adrenaline, every last bit of rage and panic and hope, into her swing.

The jacksaw sheared through the bot's polymer muscle, deep enough to hit alloy. The impact nearly jarred her shoulders from their sockets. Sparks gushed out in a torrent, blinding her goggles. She felt the saw buck in her hands, heard the scream of metal giving way, realized she was screaming just as loud.

The bot hit the floor in two pieces, thump-thump. Her goggles came clear just in time to see the front half start crawling toward the base of the incubation tank. Lemar's wrench came down from nowhere and smashed its cam in. The bot spasmed, twisting, trying to orient itself.

"Get its neck, Estima."

Estima looked up. Holli was sitting on the edge of the tank, kicking her legs. Her eyes were full of tears, and her face was smeared with snot, but her voice was perfectly calm.

"Get its neck, how it did to Jono," she said, with a hint of icy glee. "Fair's fair."

Estima had forgotten her little sister was fucking scary sometimes. She raised the jacksaw one last time, locked eyes with Lemar, who gave her a little nod, and lopped the bot's head off. It skittered across the flesh-fac floor. The rest of the bot went limp all at once; so did her arms. She barely managed to switch off the jacksaw before she dropped it. She gasped a breath. Steadied herself.

Then Holli came dropping off the tank, right into her arms, clinging to her like she hadn't since she was a baby. Estima hugged her back, all her dread dissolving, for at least a moment, into relief.

"Sorry I watched you and Lemar kiss each other," Holli mumbled. "Sorry I took a poo in the hydrofarm and now everybody has to drink it."

Estima choked on a laugh. "Oh, Holli," she said, rubbing her sister's back, inhaling the smell of her hair. "Holli, Holli. That's fucking disgusting."

*Well done, Estima.* Puck was back in her goggles, dancing on his strings. *But I'm afraid the bugbear invited friends. Everyone loves a pirate party.*

He cut her into a camfeed, something external, and when she blinked the sweat from her eyes she saw the Bad Block's shiny black machine cresting the roof of the arcology. Her stomach dropped.

*They're here for Holli. Stay where you are, and keep her safe.* Puck swiveled the camfeed, showing something too solid to be a cloud, too big to be a drone, drifting closer through an ochre sky. *We're almost to port.*

She stared at the flying thing, the proof that Puck's story, or at least the most staggering part of it, was true after all. "Holli deserves to know what's going on," she said heavily. "She deserves to know why you dragged her up here and nearly got her killed."

Puck didn't reply, but her little sister squirmed in her arms and looked up. "Are you talking to Puck the Pirate?" she demanded, incredulous. "Puck is *my* friend, not yours. You already have Lemar."

Estima was being very, very nice. Usually she never let Holli or anybody else use her goggles, but she had handed them over fully unlocked, and even wrapped up a chunk of ice from the freezer so Holli could hold it against her skinned elbow while Puck told her a scare-story. Holli was using it to clean her own goggles instead—both lenses were cracked, and she didn't know if she would be able to fix them, but she wanted the blood off anyway.

*How many custodians are there, Holli?* Puck asked, bobbing on his wires. His voice was in her earpods, but also outside it, because Estima had insisted, because she did not trust Puck to tell the story right.

"Lots," Holli said, more concentrated on getting the sticky red out of a little groove in her goggles. "Lots and lots of glitchy laggy custodians."

*Correct,* Puck said. *Because the custodian here, and the custodian in your neighboring arcology, kept having babies. Replicating over and over until the servers were full to bursting.*

Holli liked that idea. "Little baby custodians!" she cooed, rocking her goggles in her arms. "Little glitchy laggy babies!"

*For humans, replicating is a bit trickier,* Puck said. *And following the schism, sterility was rampant in both Blocks. Not enough mamas! Not enough dadas! Eventually, that means not enough babies.*

"The mamas and the dadas in the Bad Block ate them all," Holli informed him. "They make them into soup."

*Not quite,* Puck said. *But for the sake of biodiversity, each arcology was forced to steal children from the other. The custodians built infiltrator bots for that specific purpose.*

Holli looked at headless Moony.

*Sometimes, later on, they sent humans,* Puck said. *Once the humans were sufficiently indoctrinated. Once your Block thought the other was bad, and they thought the same of you.*

"They *are* bad," Holli said, frowning. "They're called the Bad Block."

*Let's table that for now, Holli. What's important is that over the centuries, the custodians forgot about the outside world. About keeping humans safe. They even forgot* why *they were playing the gene-stealing game.*

Holli was only half-listening. Estima and Lemar had finished locking the doors and covering up Jono, who was dead, and now they were wrapping the cut on Estima's calf with a bandage from the medico. The two of them kept whispering to each other. It was less interesting than kissing each other, but still made her curious.

Then Puck put something new in her goggles, a goretoon she'd never seen before: a massive spherical spaceship, crawling with construction bots, up so high the sky was a yellow haze below it.

"Is that a pirate ship?" she demanded.

*A generation ship,* Puck said. *The machine minds decided humanity's only hope was a new beginning. A blank slate in the stars. But to create a viable spacefaring population, they needed the drift. That's why the custodians became obsessed with novel genetic pathways. Mutations.* Puck's wooden face was solemn. *That's why the infiltrator bot came for you, Holli. You have something new in your cells.*

Holli felt her throat go tight. She looked at Moony again, this time at his spiny severed head, and realized he never even cared about the monkey paws. He had come to steal her cells, and that was why when Jono tried to stop him he'd chopped Jono in the neck.

*And that's why I was sent to extract you,* Puck said. *You're the last piece of the puzzle.* He did a little dance she used to like. *Hot, fresh genes! Never before seen! Straight from Holli's helices!*

Holli let her gaze drift to the tarp, where Jono was stiff and still underneath. She remembered what the flesh-fac man had said before he was dead: *not your friend, sick bastard, glitching custodian.*

"What are you, Puck?" she asked. "I don't think you're a pirate."

*Not in the traditional sense,* Puck said. *But I* was *designed with navigation in mind. The generation ship is ready, Holli. The final berth is for you.*

• • •

Chado's squad fanned out across the rooftop, clearing every generator, every antenna, every derelict garden. No sign of additional defenses, but no sign of the target, either—and the flying machine was still getting closer.

"Must be a trick, yeah?" Dox was tracking the flyer's approach through the scope of his weapon. "Something the Silent Tower built in secret."

"The people-eaters can't build for shit," Nayla said. "Their caretakers are all crazy." She darted a look in Chado's direction. "What should we do about it?"

Chado didn't know. Ever since he was born, he'd been told that the world outside the city was devastated, uninhabitable, that only his home tower and its warped neighbor still supported life. There was no sim for the arrival of non-existent outsiders. No protocol.

Then an unexpected signal flared through his tac goggles. The bugbear was still active after all—and it had escaped the heating vent. Its signal was coming from much closer now, almost directly below them, accompanied by an optic feed. Chado linked in.

The view from the bugbear's cam was fractured by damage, tilted at a strange angle, but he could make out four human figures. Three were sitting, painted bright orange by the infrared. One was immobile on the floor, slowly cooling to purplish blue. He focused in on the smallest of the seated figures, and saw a faint halo of target data.

Chado blinked the feed away. "She's close," he said. "We stick to the plan. Retrieve the target first, deal with the flyer after."

"Maybe they're here for her, too," Nayla muttered. "Whoever they are."

"They'll be disappointed, then," Chado said, unslinging his weapon.

Estima was slumped against the freezer with Lemar slumped beside her, wishing for the first time in ages that someone would tell her exactly what to do. The world had gotten too big too fast: this morning all she'd cared about was getting off, and now she had both Blocks warring over her little sister's genes and a third faction trying to put her on a colony ship and launch her into space.

"It should probably be up to your ma, right?" Lemar said, head tipped back, eyes fixed on the ceiling in order to not look at the corpse.

"Probably," Estima agreed. "But nothing's ever been up to any of us. Not really." She shifted, crinkling the bandage around her calf. The bot's blade had only grazed her, but it stung all the same. "The custodians call us pawns, Puck said. When we talk, it's pawn sounds. When we sleep, it's pawn-stop."

"Well, it's not like we did a great job when we were in charge." Lemar gave a shaky laugh. "We're the ones who wrecked the world."

"So why should we get to leave it?" Estima said. "If the machine minds can do all this—" She waved her aching arm. "If they can spend centuries building a ship, breeding a crew, why can't they just make things better here?"

Lemar nodded over at Holli, who was still wearing the borrowed goggles, leaning forward like she could push herself through the lenses. "Ask Puck, maybe."

"I don't trust Puck," Estima said. "He could have told us all this from the start, instead of doing his creepy puppet show shit. He's been talking to her almost a year, you know." She rubbed at her cheekbone, feeling guilty and impossibly tired. "I always thought it was just goggle games. I always thought she was trying to say—"

"Fuck," Lemar finished. "Yeah. I heard her once, too."

"What are you saying about Puck?" Holli had pulled the goggles off, dangling them from her little fist. Her eyes were gleaming with excitement. "He showed me the big ship. Did he show you the big ship?"

For a moment Estima wanted to snatch the grin off her sister's face, tell her none of this was a game. But then she remembered they were just moving pieces to the custodians, and possibly to Puck. Maybe Holli was ahead of the curve. Maybe the only way to stay sane was to keep everything a game.

Puck's synthetic voice blared from the goggles. "Hand them over, Holli. Your turn's done, and I need to speak to your sister."

Holli held them out, sulkily, and Estima grabbed them. She barely had the strap settled when Puck cut her into another exterior view: three armored figures, using a lance of reddish-purple light to burn their way through one of the Block's rooftop doors.

*Ion guns,* Puck said. *They've been busy bees, over there in the Bad Block. This is a lot more firepower than I anticipated.*

"Can't you stop them from up there?" Estima demanded. "Don't you have your own—ion guns, or whatever?"

*I'm a pacifist. This was meant to be a* stealth *extraction.* Puck sounded almost like Holli in one of her sulks. *I'll think of something. But staying put is no longer an option.*

Holli didn't like leaving Jono all alone in the flesh-fac, even if he was dead, but Estima had insisted and Lemar had offered to carry her piggyback, which was tempting after a long day of climbing around in vents. Now she was clinging to his neck while they hurried down the corridor, past the locked lifts. Puck was in Estima's goggles, leading the way, and Holli didn't like that either, since her big sister didn't even really know Puck.

"Emergency stairs should be just up ahead," Estima panted. "Gets us down to the fabs strip."

Of course, Holli was less and less sure *she* really knew Puck. He had lied about being a pirate, and about the pirate party waiting at the top of the Block, and probably about the noodle cup. He didn't tell funny jokes anymore, either.

"Shoulders, Holli," Lemar choked. "Hold my shoulders, not my neck."

Holli gave his neck a final squeeze, because she liked the bobbing feel of it under her arms, then relented. As far as she was concerned, they were going the wrong way. Puck was not a real pirate, but he had a real ship, big as the Block, floating up in orbit—and if Holli wanted to see it in real meat, she needed to get on the little ship, the one with balloons and solar engines.

It was annoying how the Bad Block kept messing things up: first with Moony the Mad Monkey, now with a whole ninja squad coming down through the roof.

"Here," Estima said, skidding to a stop in front of a dusty metal door. "Puck, help me with the lock."

Holli slithered off Lemar's back, squatting down to watch as her sister found the port and plugged her goggles in. Estima was still better at hacklocks than her, and so was Puck, but she had decided that was only because Estima was older and Puck was a machine. But if people got *too* old, they got worse at hacklocks, and that was why—

"Mama," Holli announced. "I smell Mama."

"Okay, Holli," Lemar said, but in the way that meant he didn't believe her. He still had his eyes on the end of the corridor, probably watching for the ninja squad so he could fight them with his hand-wrench.

It was true, though: Holli could smell the delicious warm stink her mama brought home after a long day in the fabs. She was sure Estima would recognize it, too, if she wasn't so busy unlocking the door. Holli tapped her sister on the shoulder, got ignored, then tried clambering onto them.

"Get off me," Estima said. "I've almost got it."

"You're being slow," Holli whispered in her ear, glad to be able to pester Estima again.

"Puck spooked our custodians," Estima muttered. "They changed all the locks. But it's just about—"

The door lurched open, and Holli felt her sister stiffen up all at once, heard Lemar give a big grunt of surprise. A man was standing at the top of the dark spiral stairs, pointing some kind of toy or tool at them. Holli felt a scaredy-worm wriggle in her belly. The ninja squad was even sneakier than Puck thought. Now they were going to have to either fight or run away, or she would end up being good soup for the mamas and dadas in the Bad Block.

"What are you imps doing all the way up here?" the man demanded, and as he caught more of the light from the corridor Holli saw he was wearing a coverall, not scary techy armor. He gave a familiar cough. "There's an invasion happening."

"We know," Estima said sourly.

Then someone else came barreling up the stairs, past the man, and wrapped her arms around Holli and Estima both. Holli knew they were supposed to be quiet, so she muffled her shriek of delight in a Mama-smelling armpit and hugged the rest of her as hard as she could. She only popped her head up to eyeball Lemar, who was standing off to the side looking nervous.

"Told you, Lemar," she said.

The instant they stepped foot inside the Silent Tower, Chado felt like he was in a dream. He'd always imagined the enemy arcology as more mound than building, a labyrinth of ever-tightening tunnels strewn with filth and gnawed bones. Instead, every single thing—from the feel of the corridor floors, to the shape of the directional decals on the ceiling, to the soft hum of the emergency lighting strips—was exactly as it ought to be.

Nayla summed it up well, in a disconcerted murmur. "Feels like we burned a hole all the way back to the home tower."

"It could be intentional," Chado said. "Trying to lull us. Make us feel safe." He tapped his goggles. "Stay sharp for traps."

The target was on the move again. They'd watched, through the bugbear's fractured cam, as the child and two others departed what seemed to be a food storage facility, moving with urgency. Chado had to assume they would flee downward, deeper into the Silent Tower, seeking strength in numbers. Time was of the essence.

But when he rounded the corner and recognized the blast door the trio had departed through, the door to the storage facility, he stopped.

"We should recover the bugbear's full memory," he said. "For analysis. Dox, watch the door."

Nayla frowned, but followed him inside. While she hurried to the bot's severed head, past the dead body, Chado inspected the facility. It was a standard meat farm, no different from the ones in the home tower, and it seemed to be at full production capacity—more than enough to feed a few hundred starving savages.

"They can grow plenty of meat," he said, as Nayla returned with the bugbear's memory in hand. "Same as us."

"So?" Nayla demanded. Her eyes were wild, unsettled. "I don't like this, Chado. Any of this. Let's get the target and get home."

Chado felt a wave of shame, for forgetting his squad was young and scared and depending on him. "We will," he said. "Trust the caretakers."

"Trust the caretakers," she echoed.

But there was one last thing to verify. He knelt down and peeled the tarp away from the body, and suddenly all his confusion about the Silent Tower became background noise, unimportant.

Whatever implement had been used to slice the bugbear's head from its body had nearly done the same to the dead barbarian: the man's throat was slashed so deeply Chado could see a splintered node of spinal column emerging from the gore. His stomach heaved, and Nayla took a short sharp breath that made Dox poke his head through the doorway.

When he saw the cause, he shuddered. "Fuck," he said. "They were trying to take his head off."

Chado clenched his teeth. People-eaters or not, the inhabitants of the Silent Tower were every bit as brutal to each other as they were in the stories.

"No harm to the target," Chado said. "Everyone else, we shoot to kill."

They slipped back into the dark corridor, weapons raised.

Their ma wanted to know exactly what the fuck was going on, but Estima only had time for the condensed version: machine minds greedy for novel genes, heavily armed ninja squad coming their way, airship steered by Puck the Pirate heading for the top of the Block to take Holli up into orbit. It was only that last bit that made her stop short on the stairs.

"A big ship in orbit," she said. "Covered in a whole swarm of build-bots."

Holli took it upon herself to answer. "Yes," she said, still gripping their ma's hand and beaming all innocent-like. "Up so high you can see the sky underneath."

"Yeah," Estima said. "Why?"

Puck had been uncharacteristically quiet, hopefully focused on finding a way to stop the ninja squad, but now he reappeared in her goggles bearing a wooden grimace. *I was really hoping to avoid this*, he said. *I hate awkward reunions.*

"Come on, keep moving," barked the man with the cough, who Estima was pretty sure lived on their strip. He was still wielding the soldering torch like a gun, but looked a lot less confident in it ever since she described the ninja squad burning straight through a metal door. "The Bad Block might be here for your imp, but they'll probably still take the rest of us for scrap meat."

Ma blinked, shook herself. Started down the stairs again. "We need a plan for when we get to the fabs," she said. "Once the custodians got the doors open for us, almost everyone headed down-tower. Said they'd keep taking stairs till they find a working lift." Her voice was strained. "So it'll just be us five, and the closest thing we have to weapons is that torch."

"Should've kept the jacksaw," Estima muttered. She locked eyes with Lemar, who was doing the disappear-into-the-background trick he always did when her ma was around. "Hey," she said, grabbing his big warm hand. "Don't worry about her. We have way bigger problems."

"Yeah," he said, trying and failing to grin.

"And there's no way I'd have found Holli without you," Estima added. "So she owes you." She gave his hand a squeeze, then looked back into her goggles. "Puck? You got anything that can help us beat body armor and ion guns?"

*Not on me,* Puck said. *But I might be able to fabricate something.*

"Weapons?" she prodded.

*Even if the materials were available, I wouldn't be allowed. Pacifist programming, remember?*

Estima narrowed her eyes, then lowered her voice. "What you said before, about awkward reunions. What did you mean by that?"

*Survive, and I'll tell you.*

"Oh, fuck you, Puck."

Mama had come to join the party, and that meant everything was going to be fine. She had even brought their coughing neighbor, the one who'd nearly spotted her earlier, or maybe *had* spotted her earlier, and he had brought a soldering torch Holli was hoping he would let her try. For now, she was content to hang off Mama's hand as they re-entered the fabs.

"If this works, how long will it take them to burn through the door?" Mama asked, either to Puck or Estima or both of them.

"Took them six minutes to do the one on the roof," Estima said. She was already heading for the nanoprinters, unspooling her cord to hook her goggles up, and it gave Holli a jealous twinge because her own goggles were broken still.

"That's head start enough," said the coughing neighbor. "We can keep moving down-tower, catch up with the others—"

"What good will that do?" Mama said, in the sharp voice that gave Holli a little tingle of delight whenever it got used on someone besides her. "We'll only put more folk in harm's way."

The neighbor grimaced. "The custodians will help us," he said staunchly. "They have to. It's an invasion."

"Your custodians are compromised," Puck said, staticky, projecting from Estima's goggles. "By internal decay and by the so-called Bad Block's electronic assault."

"And it's not an invasion," Estima added, plugging her cord into the base of the nanoprinter. "The ninja squad is only here for Holli."

"For my genes," Holli corrected. "Here for my genes."

"It's in all of your best interests to help me complete my extraction," Puck said, speaking through the nanoprinter now, voice loud and choppy. "Holli's in particular. You want to go, don't you, Holli?"

Holli did, and was about to say so when her mama's grip turned tight.

"Don't fucking talk to her." It was Mama's angriest voice, the one Holli had only ever heard twice, and it made her feel like she needed to pee. "You've done enough of that. I wish you'd never talked to me either."

Estima's head snapped up from the nanoprinter, and Lemar looked even more startled, putting his arm around her shoulders like he might need to protect her. But Mama was not talking to them. She was talking to Puck, and lucky for Puck he didn't have a body so he didn't need protecting. Probably.

"So you do remember." Puck's voice was quieter now. "I'm sorry things didn't work out, Ana. It wasn't my decision to cancel extraction."

Holli hated the sound of Mama's real name, which sounded so close to her regular name only not quite right, but she didn't think that was the reason Estima's mouth was hanging open. She focused as hard as she could to understand what came next.

"I waited for years for you to come back," Mama said. "For you to show me the stars again. My ma thought I was crazy, the way I wouldn't shut up about it. She asked everyone, see, but not one other imp in the whole Block had ever played with Stumpy the Starfish." Mama's other hand was clenched in a fist, so tight her knuckles were pale. "Eventually I gave in. Figured I'd made it all up."

"Your profile was remarkably close to ideal, but one specific gene never expressed as we'd hoped," Puck said. "And there were concurrent delays in the construction of the generation ship. It was decided to let the arcology roll the dice again." He paused. "Estima was a near miss.

Holli is perfect—we're particularly taken with her 0.3% uptick in folic acid absorption."

Mama made a sound between laughing and crying, and then Holli saw she *was* crying, saw tears brimming in her eyes. She did not like that. She wrestled her mama's arm, pushed her face into the small of her back, hoping to distract her even if it meant a go-away shove. Instead, Mama's fist came unclenched and reached back to stroke her head.

"There's only one way you get Holli," she said. "That's if me, and Estima, and anyone else in this fucked up city—and I mean *both* Blocks—can decide to come, too."

"Not realistic," Puck said. "Space is limited, and the entire *point* of the generation ship—"

"You've been building it for hundreds of years," Mama said. "There have to be redundancies."

"The entire point of *redundancies*—"

"Fifteen berths," Mama said. "We go with you now, come back with you for the rest. And when we come back, it's with a way to stop this fucked up game. Reset the custodians so their priority is making the Blocks a better home for everyone else."

"Five berths," Puck said.

Holli looked up at her mama, who was looking from Estima to Lemar to the neighbor who coughed. She was chewing her lip, which always meant she was doing sums in her head.

"Ten berths," she said. "And once we're in transit, you're going to be glad for it. You're going to realize just how many things genes can't account for."

There was a long silence. Ten berths meant ten spots, Holli knew. Ten spots on the big ship that would carry them off into space. Mama was looking at Estima. Estima and Lemar were looking at each other. The coughing neighbor was looking confused.

"Because there's no time for extended negotiations, I'll be flexible," Puck finally said. "Ten berths. Done."

Holli felt the tension go out of her mama's arm. "Done," she said. "Let's get to printing."

The custodians were agitated. The Opponent's viral strike had been the strongest in years, battering them, blinding them, forcing mass deletion of corrupted code. The digital war had been so fierce, so all-absorbing, that they'd managed to deploy barely half their countermeasures against the physical intrusion.

Now the Opponent's pawns had breached the arcology, and denizen 3902, one of the building's most fascinating genetic aberrations, was at risk of capture—because instead of staying hidden in the habitation strips, she had been led upward, ever upward, by an interloper.

An interloper! A foreign machine mind sequestered deep in the Blocknet, gathering data, manipulating variables, so it could steal denizen 3902 for itself.

If the Opponent were to succeed in its raid, abiding by the rules of the game, her lineage would at least continue in the other arcology, propagating further mutations. Potential targets, even, in the inevitable counter raid.

If an interloper took her, the lineage might end all together—the greedy machine wanted dam and sibling, too. It had seized full control of the fabrication center, and now the pawns, the foolish pawns, spoke of reset and rebellion. The custodians could not allow it. They would not allow it.

They reached across the city to their Opponent, and proposed the unthinkable: an alliance.

"Space, Sti?" Lemar rubbed hard at the back of his head. "As in—space. Outer space."

"I know," Estima said. "It's fucking crazy."

She didn't have to look him in the eye, because she was watching the nanoprinters work. It was almost like a dance, a beautiful and complicated one: hundreds of spindly little arms gliding and jittering in all directions, laying down layer after layer of gleaming plastic. A rubbery skeleton was starting to take shape.

"Ten spots," Lemar said. "And I mean, who gets to pick? How *could* someone pick?"

Estima didn't know. The idea of leaving the Block was dizzying enough on its own, never mind the rest of it. Everyone she'd ever met was born in the Block, everyone she'd ever met was on track to die in the Block. Now the world had expanded not just past the arcology, past the city, but all the way out into the stars. She tried to imagine them boarding the generation ship: her and Holli and their ma, Lemar and his ma and probably—

"Estima." Lemar hardly ever called her that, so she looked up. His eyes were dry, but his face was pale, and she could see the anguish all over it. "I don't think I want to go," he said.

Estima's stomach dropped out the bottom of her, how it had done when they were rocketing up the side of the Block, Lemar's wild laugh in her ear and his body tangled around hers. She looked down at the more important thing, the nanoprinters now putting finishing touches on a fierce mouth full of filed teeth.

Puck hadn't spent much time surveilling the Bad Block—just long enough to coordinate his extraction with the timing of their raid, he said, to use their viral strike as his own distraction. But it had been long enough to note a few key differences: what he called heavier indoctrination, higher dehumanization.

"Focus on this, for now," Estima said, partly to Lemar but mostly to herself. "Focus on us getting out alive."

Focus on anything other than the feeling in her chest, like someone had come up behind her heart with a jacksaw and split it all the way in two.

Everybody was talking about insulation, and it was boring, so Holli tugged free from Mama's hand and skipped down the row of nanoprinters. They were pulsing little blue lights in sequence, almost like the trails Puck used to make for her. She wanted to see what was at the end of it, and then maybe go all the way to the storage cubes and their big magnetic crane.

When she arrived at the last nanoprinter, and found a pair of fresh-fabbed goggles exactly like hers but not broken, she forgot about the crane—and decided she could forgive Puck for lying, maybe even for turning boring. The strap fit perfectly around her head. A familiar puppet was waiting in the lenses, slouched on his strings. He waved a greeting.

*Ahoy, Holli! Just you and me, how it ought to be, in a brand-new pair of goggles! I've got all your favorite netgames ready.*

"Good," Holli said. "Good, good, good." She was about to ask for the one Mama had talked about, Stumpy the Starfish, but then from outside her goggles she heard another version of Puck's voice. Louder, still speaking through the nanoprinter. "Puck?" She pulled one earpod free, perplexed. "Are you talking to me and talking to them at the same time but saying different words?"

*I'm a multitasker. And this way, I can tell you secrets.* Puck held a wooden finger up to his carved lips. *But don't tell Mama and Estima—they'll get jelly jelly jealous. Now, back to the group! The fun starts soon!*

Chado's tac goggles didn't have the sensory range of a bugbear, but the barbarians' heat trail was clear, leading to the entrance of what appeared to be a fabrication center. The doors were unlocked, either by error or design, and he motioned for Nayla and Dox to cover him while he took point. He stepped inside with his heart pounding double-time .

The darkened fabrication center was high-vaulted, cavernous, with towering stacks of storage cubes and row upon row of nanoprinters.

They were still humming warm, residual heat swallowing up the last remnants of the trail. He sighted left, right, hunting for movement in the shadows.

"Corners are clear," he reported, and heard his squad shuffle forward behind him.

Then an inhuman howling filled the air, and a figure came lurching out from behind the nearest nanoprinter. Chado barely had time to register the raised blade, the bared teeth, before the man lunged at him. He backpedaled and fired; the barbarian crumpled with a sizzling hole through his chest. But another was already rising to take his place, and the howling was louder now, echoing through the dark, a dozen voices, a hundred—

Another barbarian hurtled toward him, jerky steps, unnatural. Nayla brought them down, the beam of her weapon crackling past his face. The lightning flash illuminated the barbarian's face for a moment, still a rictus of rage, no shock or pain or anything but malice. He toppled to the floor, and the impact sound was too dull, too brittle.

Chado look back to the nanoprinters, where another barbarian stood in place waving its knife on loop. "They printed decoys!" he shouted, over the fake howling. "Dox, Nayla, ignore them! Ignore the enemy! The target must be—" He whirled back toward the entrance just in time to see the actual barbarians, swathed head to toe in the insulation that hid their heat, slipping out the unlocked doors. "Nayla!"

But Nayla was deaf to him, deaf to everything; she was still firing at the decoys, eyes wide and terrified. Dox was screaming as he strangled the trigger. Chado stowed his weapon, sprinted for the entrance. He caught a glimpse of a little girl's face—gaze hidden under goggles, teeth clamped in a wide grin—just before the doors slammed shut.

Six minutes of head start. Estima counted it down as they ran, pounding through the darkened corridors, shedding wispy insulation behind them. The shearing sound of the ion guns was still ringing in her ears, the deadly lightning flash still imprinted on her eyes. She was glad for that, glad for the wave of terror and adrenaline sweeping her down the hall, because it meant she couldn't think about anything else.

*Touching down,* Puck said. *Hurry.*

As if they weren't already. Lemar and Ma were carrying Holli in shifts, panting too hard to speak; the neighbor had finally dropped the soldering torch but he was still red-faced from exertion, hacking up phlegm every few steps. But when they hit the electric staircase that could carry them back up to the roof, Estima skidded to a stop. The stairs had reactivated, and they were moving the wrong way, churning downward.

It was the worst fucking time for a glitch.

Estima cast around for the maintenance panel, found it on the left wall. "I'll plug in," she gasped, prying it open. "Input must be—"

"Out of there, Sti," Lemar grunted, and she was barely clear when he swung the hand wrench, smashing the exposed circuitry into sparking smithereens.

The stairs shrieked to a halt. Lemar did a trade with her ma, hand wrench for Holli, and they traded a look at the same time, a *sometimes tech just needs to be smashed* look, and Estima didn't know if she loved that or hated it but it didn't matter anyway. Because Lemar was not coming, and if Estima had to pick between him and her ma and sister and space—

She didn't know. Didn't want to know. So she threw herself at the stairs, imagining the ion gun doing its slow steady work behind them, burning through the door of the fab. They clambered higher, higher, past the flesh-fac strip. The bandage around her calf was slipping, wet from either blood or sweat. Higher, higher, until her lungs were full of razors.

The stairs ended at an ancient rusty door, and Estima could see sunlight leaking through the tiny, scattered holes in the metal. She back-checked, to make sure Lemar wasn't going to come hurtling out of nowhere with his wrench, then plugged her goggles into the lock. The Blocknet was still a mess, but she could see human activity now, rumors and panic spreading in real time.

*They'll be fine,* Puck said. *We'll explain it all when we come back.*

He made short work of the hacklock, and the door screeched open.

Holli was on top of the Block—tip top, tippity top—and everything was so good she wanted to scream. The sky was bigger than it ever was in her goggles, endless dirty yellow, and way off in the distance she could see the cratered black desert, and she was going to get to see it even better soon because Puck's flying ship was ready for them.

They'd already run past the Bad Block's crawling machine, and she decided that one was a bug, and the flying ship was a butterfly. It was weird and wonderful to look at, floating just above the rooftop on its bulgy solar-skinned balloons like it weighed nothing at all. She recognized the plank leading up inside it, except it was metal instead of splintery wood, but everything else was new, new, new.

"Which part is the mizzen-mast?" she demanded, stomping her feet to help get the excitement out. "Which part is the poop-deck?"

"You can go once we're inside the thing," her mama muttered, because she didn't know Holli had been asking Puck.

*Mama's right*, Puck said. *You'll get the full tour aboard, Holli the Detail-Driven Pirate.*

Holli tugged at Mama's arm, but she wasn't moving. None of them were: Lemar, the coughing neighbor, even Estima were all standing frozen, staring at the ship. Even though it was ready and waiting, even though the ninja squad might still be chasing them. Nobody wanted to be first.

*This is why we extract young, Holli!* Puck waved his hands in exasperation. *Older humans are always having second thoughts. Third thoughts! Fourth, on occasion.* A glowing blue trail appeared in her goggles, leading all the way up the plank, into the ship. *How about we come back for them later, Holli? One more race! Up the ramp!*

Holli remembered the race up the heating vent, Puck threatening to cook her. He would say anything to make her follow the blue trails. And if she wriggled her hand free right now and ran up the plank, she was sure, in her belly, that Puck wouldn't let Mama run after her, and that they would not come back for everyone else later.

She squeezed her mama's fingers together hard enough to feel the bones, ensuring her full attention. Mama winced, looked down. Holli made her face serious.

"Stumpy the Starfish is inside," she said, which was maybe true. "And you'll get to meet him finally."

Mama did an almost-smile. She looked back at Estima and Lemar and the coughing neighbor, jerked her head toward the ship. Then she swung Holli up into her arms—it was a good day for getting carried—and they stepped onto the plank.

Everything was so good, right until a flash of lightning sizzled over their heads and scorched a smoking hole in the side of the ship.

The warning shot had burned a neat fist-sized hole through the chassis of the flying machine, and it had frozen the barbarians in their tracks. There were five of them, and in the harsh sunlight they looked nothing like the sharp-toothed nightmares they'd printed in the fabrication center. Two were around his own age, boy and girl. One was much older, bent over in a coughing fit.

The woman holding the target was in-between, maybe the same age as Chado's mother, and he could tell from how the target clung to her that she was *her* mother. Her face was scrawled in shock, because she'd thought they had more time, because she didn't know her own arcology's caretakers had turned on them.

"Get away from the flying machine," Chado ordered, motioning with his hand for clarity, in case they really did have their own Silent Tower speech. "Now."

When his squad had finally sliced their way out of the fabrication center, they'd found the corridors lit and a message scrolling in holo along the walls: *target is yours if you stop the ship stop the ship stop the ship.* They'd spent a furious minute debating if it was another trick, then they'd bypassed the stairs and gone straight to the waiting and functional lift.

"Hey. Look." It was the girl, and everything about her, from her dark hair to her sharp chin to the goggles pulled down around her neck, made it clear she was the target's sister. "Don't you want to know what's going on?"

She spoke strangely, putting stresses in odd places, but he understood every word.

"More tricks, more traps," Dox muttered—Nayla's panic in the fabrication center had made her more tentative, his had only made him angrier.

"Don't you want to know why you're all the way over here, risking your lives, to steal my little sister?" the girl demanded.

There were so many things Chado wanted to know, but he kept his finger on the trigger. "The dead man in the meat farm," he said. "What happened to him?"

"Your infiltrator bot," the girl said. She pointed to the blood-blotted tape around her calf. "It tried to kill me, too." She freed the goggles from her neck. "Your custodians don't want you to know anything. Same as ours. We're all one big flesh-fac to them." She held out the goggles. "Puck can explain it better than I can."

Estima's heart was pounding out of her chest, and she was pretty sure she could hear Lemar's, too. The ninja squad had caught up to them, all three of them with their ion guns out. Smoke was still leaking from the side of the flying ship; Ma and Holli were still halfway up the ramp, frozen for now, but she knew Holli could start squirming or shouting any second.

Estima was trying her best to keep eye contact with the leader, who up close, in sunlight, didn't look much older than her or Lemar. She was trying her best not to get them all shot.

"The custodians are the reason our towers don't talk," she said. "The reason we look dark and empty on all your cams, and you on ours. It's all games. All lies."

The leader stared at her through his own dark goggles, and it was impossible to tell what he was thinking—his fine-boned face was so motionless it could have been a mask. The two behind him were a lot more forthcoming.

"Has to be a trick, Chado," the jumpy one said. "Viral load in those goggles, I bet."

"Maybe," murmured the other. "Maybe not."

Then all three of them jolted at once; Estima saw something flash through their goggles and heard a tinny clamor of synthesized voices—if it was loud enough to hear in the air, it must have been deafening inside their earpods. She stared in confusion, wondering if this was Puck's pacifist version of a weapon, if he was giving them a chance to run for it.

The transmission increased in volume, bringing one of the ninja squad to their knees, and Estima heard the words pumping into their ears: *kill the pawn she is corrupted kill the pawn trust the caretakers kill the pawn stop the ship trust the caretakers.*

Lemar tensed beside her, raising the hand-wrench. Estima's stomach was in freefall again, but the voices had already vanished, the squad were already shaking their heads clear, and there was no way anyone was getting out alive once they started shooting.

She grabbed Lemar's arm. "Wait," she said, and then to Ma and Holli and the terrified neighbor. "Wait."

All three of their pursuers were upright again, weapons aimed.

"The order's clear," the jumpy one muttered.

But the leader didn't move.

"Fucking custodians," Estima said, loud, in case their eardrums were pulped. "Fucking caretakers. Always glitching, right?" She swallowed hard, and made a guess. "Always short on the water ration. Always rescheduling the load shedding last minute."

The calmer one gave a twitch, maybe recognition.

"We used to tell scare-stories about you, when I was younger," Estima said, holding tight to Lemar's arm. "Said people from the Bad Block had their eyeballs plucked out and stuck cams in the holes instead."

The leader lowered his weapon lowered by a centimeter. "Ours said you had razors for teeth."

Estima shook her head. "Nah. Nah. Holli can bite pretty hard, though." She peeled her lips back. "There's my teeth," she said. "Your turn."

"Stalling, Chado," the jumpy one said. "Tricks, traps—"

The leader named Chado lifted his gloved hand, and his squad-mate went quiet. Estima waited, breath bated. Then slowly, very slowly, Chado peeled his goggles away from his face. He had sucker marks, just like Holli at the end of the day, and his eyes were fully intact. Fully human.

"Weapons down, Dox," he said. "Nayla." His squad-mates complied, one more grudging than the other. He peered at her, blinking in the sudden sunlight. "Who do we trust, then?" he asked.

Estima gave what was either a winning grin or a horrible grimace. "Start with me," she suggested. "Then, you know, feel it out."

The leader looked down at his goggles, turning them over in his hands. Then he dropped them, and brought his heel down on the lenses with a squealing crunch. Holli, still wrapped in their ma's arms, gave an affronted howl.

Estima offered him her own goggles again, and just before he took them she heard Puck's faint voice. "Excellent work, Estima. You have a real knack for talking to humans."

Puck said the flying ship was tiny compared to the one waiting in orbit, barely a rowboat, but it seemed big enough to Holli and she was determined to explore every bit of it. All the machinery looked different from the stuff in the Block, and the metal floors shone different, and the air even smelled different—and every time she passed the window, saw the real ground way down below, the city fading out of sight behind them, her stomach gave a little happy-worm wriggle.

Mama had spent a long time hugging Estima and giving her compliments, which Holli never liked, but now she was speaking in low voices with the coughing neighbor, and Estima and Lemar had drifted away to the back of the ship, probably to kiss. Holli decided it would be okay to sneak up on them, just this once, because it was part of the exploring.

"Hush, Puck," she whispered, even though he hadn't been talking much. "I'm sneaking."

*Oh, Holli! An eavesdropper after my own heart!* Puck was in a good mood, dancing on his strings. *You know I was joking, before. When I told you to bite Mama's hand and go up into the ship without her.*

"I know, Puck," she lied.

*It all worked out for the best, in my opinion,* Puck said. *No better way to strengthen a crew than a few pre-existing vicinal and familial bonds, and besides—a good captain never leaves a man behind. That's what I always say.*

"You never say that," Holli said. "Hush."

Puck wiped his mouth away, leaving nothing but smooth wood, and Holli made for the back of the ship. It looked a lot like their apartment back in the Block, right down to the folding bed clinging to the wall.

Estima and Lemar were tucked into the little nook behind it, and their legs were tangled up, because they had long legs and no space, but they were only talking.

"One day, and everything changes forever," her sister said.

"One really long day," Lemar said, resting his head against the wall. "Yeah."

"Ten spots," Estima said. "That's enough for your ma. Your aunt."

Lemar grimaced. "What about their ten, Sti? And those folks' ten?"

"Not everyone will want to—" Estima cut herself short. Did one of her shaky breaths, like she might cry. "You really don't. You really don't want to come with me."

"I do," Lemar said, looking pained. "I want to come with you, go with you, be with you. All things with you. But if it goes wrong—"

"Things are always going wrong."

"If it goes wrong between *us*," Lemar said, in a trembly voice. "How it did for your parents, and my parents, then what?"

Estima was quiet for a long time, then she reached over and put her hand on Lemar's hand. "Then we'll be neighbors," she said. "Exactly how we'd be in the Block. Really good neighbors."

Lemar blinked. Then he smiled, and Holli could almost see why Estima liked his face so much. "So it'd be a near miss," he said. "Just your style."

"Second best forever," Estima said, rolling her eyes in the way Holli was still getting the hang of.

"Fuck that," Lemar said, and then they finally started kissing, and Holli only let herself watch for a few seconds before she crawled away.

*I was rooting for those two,* Puck said, once they were out of Lemar and Estima's earshot. *High hormonal chemistry, solid psychological compatibility.*

"When can I tell everyone the secret, Puck?" Holli demanded.

"What secret?"

Holli blinked, looked up, saw Mama standing against the window, arms folded. "Mama," she said. "You snuck up on me."

"I learned it from you," Mama said, in her dry, dry voice. "What secret?"

*You might as well,* Puck said. *Given her aggressive negotiating earlier, I think she already suspects.*

Through the bit of window beside her mama's hip, Holli saw a towering structure emerging in the dusty distance, taller than the Block and the Bad Block combined. Puck said it was a skyhook, even though it looked nothing like the pirate hooks he'd put on her hands this morning. He said when it was time to go on the generation ship, it would toss them all the way up into orbit.

Holli grinned up at her mama. "Once we're on the big ship, Puck is going to be the first mate," she said. "And I'll be something else."

Mama's eyes widened. Her mouth tightened. "Once we're on the ship," she echoed. "How far off is that?"

"Guess what I'll be, Mama," Holli sang. "Guess what I'll be, Mama!"

*Sailing the stars, scouring the nebulae, in the grand and gallant search for terra nova!* Puck jigged on his strings. *The inimitable, the implacable . . .*

## ABOUT THE AUTHOR

**Rich Larson** (*Ymir, Tomorrow Factory*) was born in Galmi, Niger, has lived in Spain and Czech Republic, and is currently based in Grande Prairie, Canada. His fiction has been translated into over a dozen languages, among them Polish, French, Romanian and Japanese, and his *Clarkesworld* story "Ice" was adapted into an Emmy-winning episode of *LOVE DEATH + ROBOTS.*

# The Arborist

## DERRICK BODEN

Through the cracked, moldering ribs of the alien planet sprouted a life reborn. Or something similar. Mealy stalks of bone white vegetation, thorns like scythes, a whole forest—a whole *world*—of ashen rootstocks clawed at the helium-purpled sky, gnawing at itself like ingrown toenails. The tree that was also a forest grew, and the planet died. Right on schedule.

Almost.

Pele walked among it, uncertain. The tree (what a strange thing for the humans to call it, Pele thought—this vast solitary organism, imported from Earth, that embraced the entire planet of Iona) had performed admirably. Its job was nearly done; soon, it would rest. And so would Pele. The stasis ships would arrive in a matter of weeks, welcomed to a planet devoid of the horrors that had so recently throttled it. A fertile planet, grown from the rotting husk of the tree itself—and from that which it had overcome. The refugees would have a home, thanks to their tree. And, in some small way, thanks to Pele.

There was only one problem.

Pele dropped into a narrow gully beneath a canopy of lifeless vines. A whole host of dead things crunched underfoot: the desiccated skull of a vulturaptor, its eighteen-inch serrated beak riddled with spore-holes; the vine-wrapped carcass of a leech bear; a whole legion of fat-bodied fang grubs. Pele's soft-cell optics captured evidence of the carnage in still-frame images, archived in solid-state memory in the base of Pele's carbon fiber skull. The carnage itself was fine, Pele reminded itself dutifully, even as the android cringed at the grime worming into the weather-worn skin seams along its knee joints. It was what lay *beneath* that was the problem: the depth at which Pele's booted foot sank into the remains of the tree itself.

A certain amount of rot was expected. The tree was meant to die, after all, to lay groundwork for fresh soil and—ultimately—human crops. The problem was how fast it was dying. The decay had not yet reached an alarming pace, but the pace was *accelerating*. This was a tenuous time in the tree's lifecycle; if it decayed too rapidly, it would leave the door open for any surviving endemic life—a murdermite swarm, a colony of jackrabids, a single bone eater—to wrestle back from the brink of extinction.

This, on the eve of the refugees' arrival, would be disastrous. The refugees were largely defenseless: Iona's endemic life would show no mercy.

So, with the assistance of Yui's enigmatic clues, Pele had been searching for answers. In the arid flatlands of the Sun Belt, throughout the frigid North Isles, across the mainland's diverse girth. And here: in the muggy tropics where the air clung to Pele's silicone skin and clogged its thermal-regulating pores, where Pele knelt gingerly—and, it hoped, respectfully—amongst all those vicious bodies, to collect samples from a pulpy rhizome in the ruptured earth.

Pele shivered only a little at the grit that congealed between its fingers, grit that—not long ago—Mal would've fretted over, scrubbed clean with a long-handled toothbrush in the predawn light. The android inserted the sample into a pocket analyzer, then scaled the gorge in long, easy lunges. Every third stride, Pele's left knee hitched slightly where Mal had rewired the articulation after the mishap with the vulturaptor—a jury-rig while the 3D printers were tied up with shuttle repairs, then station repairs, then everything else. Pele did not mind: the hitch reminded the android of Mal's unfaltering compassion (*your knee is totally off-grid now, Pele*). Up top, Pele took a moment to soak in the view. The alien sun made ragged stab wounds of the marine layer. The tree-forest was gnarled and pale and deathly still. To the west, a broken trunk with the girth of a small city rose some two-hundred meters into the sky.

*What do you see when you look at it?* Mal had asked.

"I see inevitability," Pele said aloud, though did not know what to make of its own answer. Nor could the android expect any guidance in the matter. Mal was long gone, as was the Commander. And Biggs, still comatose. Only Yui remained, and she—

The analyzer chimed. Pele scanned the cramped screen. A direct data feed would've been far more efficient, but these devices were meant for human hands and eyes. Pele was only filling in. Halfway down the screen, Pele's optics lingered on a single word: *abnormality*.

The android made for the shuttle without delay.

• • •

Following a much-needed decontamination, Pele disembarked onto Watcher-1 through the primary vestibule. It wasn't protocol for a nonhuman to use Primary, but it had been three months since anyone but Pele had ventured out by shuttle, and eventually decorum had ceded to efficiency. There was no one around to disagree.

Or, rather, there *hadn't been*.

"What are you *doing*?"

Pele froze halfway through the interior airlock portal. "Lieutenant Biggs. You're awake."

Biggs leaned heavily against the mudroom wall, struggling with the buttons of his tunic. Underneath, his generally toned muscles had lost definition during his time in the infirmary. Irritated, he said, "Why are you so surprised?"

*Because*, Pele didn't reply, *the automedic assured me I had another week*.

"I'm happy to see you," Pele said.

Biggs eyed him. Now did not seem the best time to mention the abnormality. So Pele said nothing. Biggs abruptly made for command.

Over his shoulder, "Status."

Pele hustled to keep up. "Watcher-1 is presently cruising at fifteen-thousand meters—"

"I don't care about the damn station." Biggs squeezed through the ingress to command. It was a small room, just a few meters across. Also, as ever, vacant. Disappointment flashed in Biggs' eyes. "Where the hell is everyone?"

Pele hesitated at the entrance. Protocol did not permit a nonhuman to enter command uninvited. Biggs hammered at the touchscreens with a rigid finger.

"Get the hell in here. Who remapped these controls, who—?" Biggs spun, glared. "What *happened*?"

The sudden rush of human activity, albeit from a single person, left the android floundering between the desire to convey information and the fear of inciting panic. How much did Biggs remember of the incident? Pele said, "Commander Nuñez and Yui had a disagreement, which resulted in—"

"I know Nuñez is dead." Biggs ran his hand across the dark skin of his scalp, all the way to the marbled scar at the back where shrapnel from the blown fuel canister had robbed him of three months of his life. "I'm groggy, not an idiot. Where's—" He bit off whatever he was about to say. "Where's Mal?"

Through the 270-degree dome window, a gauzy cirrus layer stretched to the curved horizon. Much further, not yet visible to the station's optical instrumentation, nine stasis ships screamed toward them at a tenth the speed of light.

Pele remembered Mal's boyish features, her eager eyes, her relentless questions. *What will they think of this place in a hundred years? Will anyone know what happened? Will you tell them?*

"Mal is gone." Pele studied Biggs' reaction. "To the planet's surface."

"Where? For how long?"

"I do not know. Since shortly after the incident. We have had no luck locating her: it is possible her shuttle veered into an electromagnetically-shielded region, such as the equatorial trench." Or, she'd manually disabled the shuttle's transponder—but Pele had no desire to provoke Biggs' suspicions by offering this hypothesis.

Biggs was not expecting this. "And . . . Yui?"

"She is here."

He reached for the comms panel on the wall. "Why didn't you say so?"

"She is self-isolating."

Biggs froze. "Explain."

"She . . . " Pele glanced out the window, for courage, but the tree was concealed by clouds. "She does not leave her quarters. We communicate via the comms terminal."

What Pele did not say, was that Yui *did* leave her quarters during the graveyard hours, while Pele recharged—though she never left the station. Pele did not say this, because Pele did not understand what it meant, and because Pele knew Yui would not appreciate if the android divulged her habits.

Biggs steadied himself against the wall. "So what you're saying is, everything has gone to hell."

He didn't even know about the tree.

Biggs eyed Pele sidelong. "Where were you?"

"I was collecting samples on the surface."

Biggs glanced at the analyzer on Pele's hip. "What did you find?"

"The abnormal rate of decay has accelerated."

Biggs' eyes widened a fraction. He glanced over his shoulder: at the unseen ships, Pele knew, where his partner and children breezed ever-closer, in stasis. "And what has been done to stop it?"

"I am still gathering data."

"You're—" Biggs struggled contain his anger. "This is everything, Pele. We cannot waste time *gathering data*. Yui should've—wait. You've been collecting samples . . . alone?"

"I have been doing everything alone."

Biggs gripped Pele's shoulders, turned Pele to face the egress. Pele registered with mild alarm his back panel sliding open. "I'm going to run some tests."

"I maintain a rigorous diagnostic routine—"

"Checks and balances." Biggs fiddled with Pele's subdermal touchscreen. "Nothing personal."

Pele understood. For Pele to perform independently, a certain amount of internal autonomy was necessary. This autonomy came with risks. This was among the chief reasons why Watcher-1 did not maintain a wholly automated crew during the gardening phase of the migration. It certainly would've been easier: they'd sacrificed considerable resources to send even this small of a task force. But their mission was too important for it to go unsupervised.

"I'm going to shut you down for a little while." Biggs worked the controls with a degree of uncertainty; he was still groggy. Likewise, emotional. Pele experienced a mounting dread. If Biggs so chose, he could wipe Pele's memory in seconds. Everything the android had experienced on Iona: the landing, the tree, Mal. It was irrational to think Biggs would do such a thing—Pele's memories were the only contiguous history upon which the crew could rely, anymore—but the android could not shake the sudden concern. Biggs continued, "Download your findings, make sure you're clean. Once Yui comes out—"

"She will not come out."

Biggs paused, his fingers embedded in Pele's back. "On the comms, then."

"She . . . might not respond to you."

Biggs kept his fingers on the touchscreen. Pele wondered: had it chosen these words out of self-preservation? Or was it simply doing its job? Did humans question their autonomy so routinely?

Biggs closed the panel, spun Pele around. "But she'll respond to you."

There was an edge to Biggs' voice. His relationship with Yui had always been complicated, even by human standards.

"Perhaps," Pele said.

Biggs slumped into a chair. "Get her on the line."

It took nearly seven minutes. Finally, Yui's face fuzzed into view on the display. Her hair was unkempt, like a nest of black straw, as always. She looked deeply unhappy. As always.

"Pele, it's early—" Her eyes flicked to the background, to Biggs. Her expression went frigid. "Biggs."

"Yui."

A lengthy silence followed.

"Well." Yui glanced away. "This has been fun and all, but—"

"It's been three months," Biggs said. "The hell have you been doing?"

"Your job," Yui said, to which Biggs glanced not-very-subtly in Pele's direction. "With Pele's help, thanks bud. It hasn't been a vacation, if that's what you're implying."

Biggs sat up sharply. "It isn't meant to be."

"Well then, mission accomplished."

"Mission accomplished? From what I'm told, it's been the exact opposite. Must I remind you," said Biggs. "We're doing this for our families."

"No, we're doing this for *your* family."

Biggs swallowed his first response. Yui's own kin had all fallen to the plague. Their memory had once served as her primary motivation. But this place had changed her, as it had changed them all. Biggs said, "We're doing this for all of them."

"Your tree is a plague. It shouldn't be here, and neither should we."

Yui's appraisal surprised Pele, though the organism's dubious origins were no secret.

"There's nowhere else to go! Earth is an irradiated corpse. Ninety-seven exoplanets in habitable zones within range of the fleet, ninety-six of them devoid of viable atmosphere. We don't have the time or resources for that kind of terraforming. What should we do? Stuff the entire surviving population under a dome for the next thousand years? There's water here, breathable air. This is our *only choice*."

She looked away. He was losing her.

Biggs didn't seem to notice. "It's our sworn duty."

"I walked a kilometer in your shoes," said Yui. "Or Nuñez's maybe. You know what I learned? Watching a planet die fucking *blows*."

Biggs was standing, now. "It is not dying. The invasives are vicious, hateful, even toward themselves. You want to be eviscerated by a vulturaptor, is that it? Jesus, you sound like Mal."

It was not a fair assessment, Pele knew. Mal had always been the optimist. The *idealist*, as the Commander had so often chided: the only one who'd rebuffed his insistence on referring to Iona's endemic life as *invasives*.

Yui fell silent. She was about to hang up. Pele made a subtle motion to Biggs, who rubbed his face.

"Pele told me about Mal." Biggs stepped closer to the screen, dropped his voice. "I'm going to find her, Yui."

"Good luck with that."

The screen went dark.

"As you surmised," Pele said, "things have indeed gone to hell."

Biggs stared out the window. "Get that sample to the autolab. There'll be no rest tonight. Tomorrow we go to the surface."

They dropped a hundred kilometers south of the equatorial trench, in the vast wetlands. The air was thick and hot; they sloshed through bog water that was knee-deep at its shallowest point. Dead things disintegrated messily underfoot. Pele fretted silently about silicon seal-seams and corrosion.

Out loud, the android said, "I have a curated list of high-risk locations. It should prove more efficient than random—"

"If your list was any good." Sweat streamed freely down Biggs' scalp, dripped from the end of his rebreather. "You'd have fixed the problem already."

The tree's tendrils rose from the murky water like overgrown mangroves, scratching at the overcast sky. Such a lonely life, Pele thought: blasted from Earth in that hardened spore pod, preceding even this small team of gardeners by a dozen years. How far it had traveled to wage this war and, ultimately, to die. They had been through much together, Pele and the tree.

"Perhaps you give me both too little and too much credit: the list has turned up traces of the abnormality, though identifying a problem and resolving it are two entirely different—"

"Besides." Biggs pushed through a thick mass of vines. "This location isn't random."

Pele followed Biggs through. A floodplain stretched before them for kilometers. The water was perfectly still, besides the ripples that fled from their own bodies. Here, the tree was sparse: an occasional bone-white column punched through the water like teeth through a broken gumline.

Biggs sloshed to the nearest tooth. Pele kept pace. It felt like an intrusion, the turbulence they caused in the water. Again, Pele remembered Mal.

*You know who's got it right, Pele? Ghosts. Travel here and there, never leave a trace.*

In Biggs' grip, the upthrust stalk crumbled to ash. He gave Pele a significant look, because of course the tree was not meant to crumble to ash, not yet. Every detail of its lifecycle had been painstakingly engineered. Time-locked catalysts within the tree produced enzymes that caused it to rapidly decay into proto-soil, while unlocking a multitude of secondary organisms—bacteria, insects, early-stage crops—in preparation for humanity's arrival. But those catalysts had not yet been delivered.

Pele collected samples with a neoprene-gloved hand. "How did you choose this place?"

Biggs eyed Pele sidelong. "A hunch."

Meaning, perhaps, Biggs didn't want to say. But why would Biggs not trust Pele? And was he right to do so? It had been three months. The instructions that Yui had left around the station, Pele had followed to the letter. The android cared deeply for the tree, tended to it with unwavering care.

Yet Pele was not human. Trust came grudgingly, at best.

Biggs looked away. Pele watched his reflection in the flattening water. His brow was knotted, his eyes dark with worry.

Pele moved closer, slowly as to minimize disruptions in the water. "You fear what will come of your family."

Biggs' shoulders caved. He looked so vulnerable, a lone man on this desolate marsh, trillions of kilometers from home. "You saw this place before. If the invasives are permitted to regain even the slightest foothold . . . life is too horrific." He did not specify *life here*, Pele noticed. "We will all die. My daughters, my son . . . "

He stopped, incapable of finishing the thought.

Pele burned a few cycles considering how to respond.

Biggs' wrist-comms buzzed.

"The sweep is done." He glanced at his wrist, frowned. "I'll be damned."

Pele waited for him to elaborate. Instead, Biggs squeezed his earlobe and said, "Yui, stand by for coordinates." Then, after a moment, "I found Mal."

The cave was shallow and labyrinthine. Its arteries plunged into the hard clay of the equatorial trench wall, splitting and reconnecting countless times. At its heart, near enough to the surface for Iona's pale afternoon light to worm its way inside, lay a chamber some ten meters across. Squat pylons had been set up along the perimeter; some at the back still appeared to be functional—whatever *function* that may be—green LEDs merrily flashing. The ones at the front had been toppled and, in some cases, mauled. Between the pylons sprawled the aftermath of a terrible battle.

The battle was not dissimilar to that which had transpired across the whole of the planet. It was tree versus endemics, pale fingers of rootstock twined vise-tight around the lifeless husks of a dozen sickleshrooms, interspersed with the putrefying bodies of jackrabids and bone eaters and muggermoths. Only, in the cave all of this had happened quite recently. Within the week, by the still-smooth sheen of the sapling growths and the acrid scent of the tree toxins that had likely finished off the predators. Somehow—Pele glanced suspiciously at the flashing pylons—this place had very nearly managed to evade the tree's impartial judgment.

"What the Earth-loving *fuck*?"

Biggs stood at the center of the chamber, rebreather affixed to his face, staring at the ground. Or rather, something *on* the ground. His eyes were wide, his lips contorted. Pele resented everything about this moment. The android tiptoed around the myriad carcasses, careful not to disturb a stray bone or strip of lingering flesh.

Biggs was already looking toward the entrance, where Yui leaned against the rough clay wall, her body cast in silhouette by the stubborn light from outside. "You see?" he said. "Everything here wants to kill us."

When Pele looked down at Mal's face, an unpleasant recalibration percolated through the android's systems. Perhaps this was what humans called *grief*.

Mal's body was largely intact. Based on the rate of decay in Iona's bacteria-sparse atmosphere, she'd been dead for about two weeks—a few days longer than the tree had been present in this cave. This lent credence to Pele's suspicions that the pylons were hers, employed as a means of keeping the tree at bay and, in turn, keeping the endemics in the cave safe.

But *why*? Pele had no answer.

By the state of Mal's clothing and the quantity of expended supplies in the corner of the cave, she'd managed to survive alongside some of the endemics for a number of weeks before the inevitable had happened. The sickleshroom growth had entered her torso from a point between her scapula, gestated in her lungs and burst through her ribcage into a towering stalk of vibrant orange fruitbodies. The shroom spores had left her mercifully comatose throughout the process; her expression was placid, emotionless.

Biggs pointed at Mal's corpse. "Everything *everywhere* wants to kill us. That's *life*, Yui. This is why we fight."

The backlighting obscured Yui's reaction. She leaned against the rock, rebreather tube dangling awkwardly, as if she didn't know what to do with her own body. It was her first trip off-station since the incident. Mal had been her lover for some time, back then. Strange, Pele thought, that Biggs' sweep had found Mal so quickly once he'd switched to the L-band microwave scanners they used to monitor subsurface endemic colonies. Yui had access to all the same equipment; had she even looked? Or had she known where Mal had gone all along?

Pele studied the sickleshroom protruding from Mal's chest. It was dead now, too, strangled by a single thread of winding rootstock before the sickleshroom had managed to infest the rest of Mal's corpse. Life, feeding on life, feeding on life.

"Inevitability," Pele whispered.

"Exactly," Biggs said, misunderstanding. "What a waste. She had to know what would happen! We saw the early expeditions, the cohabitation failures. We are *prey* here. This kind of reckless—" He broke off, sudden shock in his eyes. "Could she have engineered the virus?"

Pele was at a loss. "Virus?"

"The anomaly," Biggs said impatiently. "Autolab says it's a virus. Could she have built it?"

Strange, that Biggs had not shared these findings with the android. Again, Pele wondered: why would Biggs not trust Pele? And why, if his confidence ran so thin, had Biggs not reformatted Pele as he'd previously threatened? The android suspected that it owed its longevity to Yui: she would never forgive Biggs for reformatting Pele, and Biggs could not afford to lose any more personnel to internal squabbles.

"Unlikely," Pele said. "She had very little equipment, no laboratory. By what we've seen here, her objective was purely observational." Despite her disagreements with the Commander, Mal had never opposed the mission, nor the tree itself: her objectives has *always* been observational. "Without contradicting evidence, it would be prudent to assume that a viral outbreak was the result of naturally-occurring factors—"

"We'll see," said Biggs.

Yui turned away. "I'm going back to the ship."

Biggs started to follow her, forced himself still. Pele, still crouching, lingered near Mal's face. Her cheeks were sunken; her irises were cloud-pale. In the diffuse light, her skin looked transparent.

Like a ghost.

Two days later, Pele carried the body bag through the halls of the station with the solemn deliberation of a mourning parent. The halls were narrow, forcing Pele to walk sideways or risk bumping Mal's body. It was slow going - especially considering the delicate condition of the body, which they'd fumigated and flash-frozen to eliminate any traces of endemic life the tree hadn't already snuffed out. The resulting corpse looked very little like Mal, and Pele was glad for the bag, if not for the antiquated custom of preserving the remains of the dead. Biggs' voice carried through the station in brusque, metallic echoes. He'd been digging through the system logs since their return from the surface for signs of *human intervention*.

Which, Pele noted, might summarize the whole of their mission.

"Goddamn spaghetti code," he said. "If Yui would help in the slightest . . . "

Approaching the clean room, Pele slowed. Through the plex windowpane, the autolab hunched beneath pale orange lights. The sample repository, Pele noticed, was empty. The nearby biofab, a boxy black machine on squat legs, flashed *PROCESSING*. Biggs had been busy; he'd hardly slept since waking from the coma.

"What we need," Biggs was saying, "is a pattern analyzer that isn't complete junk."

Pele entered cold storage. The chamber was small, cluttered with frozen rations and canisters of liquefied gas, a dismal place to house the dead. But the station had no proper morgue—a decision made to improve morale or to save space, Pele did not know—so Pele slid Mal into the storage rack alongside the bagged body of Commander Nuñez.

The bags were opaque, the contents similarly sized: the hand-printed tags along the bottom were their only differentiator. The station's refrigeration units would prevent decomposition until the fleet had arrived and its occupants had determined how best to honor those who had given their lives for the salvation of humankind.

And how would they be remembered? As they had begun their tenure on Iona, loyal and fearless stewards to humanity's future? Or as they had ended it, fractured and disparate?

"I miss him."

Biggs' voice came from unexpectedly close, at the chamber's entrance. Pele turned to see his face drawn.

"Strange that I would," he continued. "I've been in a coma since the accident. But seeing him here, my heart knows how long he's been gone. I miss his level head."

Laughter filled the hallway. Biggs reddened, turned to face Yui, who said, "That's bullshit and you know it. The guy was nuts."

Biggs put his palms to his temples. "The impending failure of the mission isn't enough to drag you out of your cave—" He winced at his choice of words. "But ridiculing the dead is?"

"Nuñez was completely unhinged," she said. "How could you not see that?"

"Easy." Biggs' jaw was trembling. "I respect the chain of command."

"Your *chain of command* threw a punch at a defenseless subordinate over his bullshit idolatry."

"He found endemic samples in Mal's quarters. She could've sunk the whole operation!" Then, quieter, "After what we saw in that cave, maybe she did."

"It was a handful of spores in a sealed tank. She's—she *was*—a scientist. Of course she was curious. And he went *apeshit*."

"Speak for yourself," Biggs said darkly.

"I did what I had to do for Mal. Can't say the same for you." Of course, Biggs *had* eventually tried to intervene—and had wound up in a coma as a result. "Nuñez was nuts. You should've seen his quarters."

"Funny," said Biggs. "That's my next stop."

Yui was clearly not expecting this.

Pele, who had eagerly remained silent until then, said, "The Commander's quarters are private domain—"

"Mission objectives supersede decorum." To Yui, Biggs said, "We need his command codes to deploy the fertilizer. We're going to use it to distribute the antiviral, once the biofab is done synthesizing it."

Incredible, Pele thought, how much Biggs had accomplished in a few short days, while Pele had struggled to even acquire a sample of the abnormality for testing.

Yui shook her head with open disgust. "And you can't enter his quarters without a joint override. You know Biggs, most of the time a person needs a favor, they ask."

Biggs looked away. "Yui, listen. I'm—"

"Forget it." She made for Commander Nuñez's quarters. "Let's go. It'll do you good to see this."

Commander Nuñez's bed was immaculate, corners tucked under the mattress and pillow gently fluffed. His nightstand held nothing but a small lamp; his dresser was tidy and sparse: a single framed photograph in the corner, four smiling faces under a long-distant sun. If Pele were to have judged by this side of the room, the Commander would've seemed a simple, contented man.

Then there was the other side.

The thing Pele saw first, and last, was the mural. It was massive, sprawling, a chaotic snarl of etched lines that at first seemed to defy any pattern whatsoever. But there *was* a pattern—a picture, in fact, and much more—that only took shape after Pele had stared at it for some time. Much like the thing it depicted, its contours were varied and contrasting, its girth all-encompassing, its complexity almost impossible to grasp.

Biggs said, "Is that . . . ?"

Yui nodded. It was the tree, sprouting from a curved horizon, stretching up and out through the tenuous atmosphere, its space-borne talons grasping at one planet after the next, toward a distant asymptote. Although the horizon was clearly meant to depict Iona, it was not the origin of this vast interstellar entity. To the far left, where the wall met the adjoining terrace of built-in shelves, was depicted another planet from which its own talon stretched. The disposition of this planet's continents were unmistakable. Earth. Within the margins of the planet from which humanity had fled were etched words: *from ash and bone it seeds, our true god Yggdrasil, shepherd to this promised land and again . . .*

The Commander's imagery was at least partially grounded in fact, Pele noted. The tree *had* been developed from the same genetic core as the bioengineered plague that had throttled the Earth, leaving only ash and radiation and the displaced remnants of humanity. The irony was not lost on Pele, that they'd invested all their hope in an adaptation of the very thing that had imperiled them from the start. But they were, if nothing, desperate.

On the floor near the mural sat dozens of objects that Pele could only categorize as *sacrifices*. A tarnished silver ring, a baby's scuffed shoe, a ticket stub to some long-forgotten musical. Paraffin candles, chalk sketches in bright yellows and blues, photographs so faded they might've seen years in the Commander's pocket. The faces of his family, all of them victims of the plague.

"You'd think he'd have hated the thing," Yui said, perhaps speaking from experience. "After what it did to his family. Instead, he worshipped it."

Biggs said nothing. Pele stared at the mural. The imagery affected the android deeply, though it could not say why.

"Come on," Yui said. "Look at this shit. Old Norse mythology? Dude was a nut. You should read his journal, all Father, Son, and Holy Tree—"

"Or maybe you *shouldn't* have," Biggs said. "A person is entitled to their beliefs."

"Is that right?" Yui was in his face, now. "And what about Mal? What about her beliefs?"

"Her beliefs were treasonous! Nihilistic. If not for Nuñez, she would've brought the same fate to us that she brought on herself."

Yui bared her teeth. "Nuñez worshipped a fucking plague tree."

"Pele." Biggs was flushed with anger. "What's the probability of successful human habitation on Iona while endemic life persists?"

Pele stood in the doorway, hoping to sublimate into the HVAC.

"You don't have to answer that," Yui said.

"Answer!" shouted Biggs. "How long will humanity survive here if we fail?"

It would've been nice to be on the surface at that moment. There was a place in the north where the air shimmered like a vast prism when it rained. "Our models estimate an open-air human colony of our current technological aptitude would be eradicated within four months, should endemic life return to ten percent of its prior state."

"So the 'invasives' die, so what?" said Yui. "You think that's it?"

"It's a necessary first step," said Biggs.

"And then what? What if the degeneration doesn't progress? What if Terran life refuses to grow, and we're left with another barren rock—this one by our own design? Or worse: what if the tree refuses to die, just like its predecessor? I've seen what it can do, on Earth and now here. The scope of death is . . . it's too much to take. It's a *plague*." She wasn't looking at Biggs anymore, but at a point somewhere distant, a place only she could see. "They say they fixed it, but what if they're wrong? What if this time it drags us to our graves for good?"

"Then at least we tried."

Yui threw up her hands, stormed out. Her footsteps faded behind Biggs' heavy breathing. Pele picked at detritus lodged in its knuckle-seams.

Biggs watched the android, darkly. "It wasn't an accident, was it Pele?"

If only Mal were here. If only they were on the surface. In the tropics, the rapid decomposition of endemic algae had left a twenty-kilometer slick of phosphorescence on the delta that glowed as brightly as the milky way on a moonless night.

Biggs stepped closer. "When Yui struck that hydrogen canister, the angle had to be *just right* for it to take off Nuñez's head."

Once, at night, moving in opposition to every one of its self-preservation routines, Pele had waded into the delta. The feeling of standing there, aglow amidst all that decay, had been transcendent.

"She murdered him," Biggs said. "Admit it."

*Everything everywhere wants to kill us.* "It is possible."

"I'm locking her in her quarters." Biggs said this on his way out, though he only reached the doorway before the alarm stopped him dead.

"Command codes accepted," the station announced, "aerial transport deployed."

Biggs glanced at the desk, where moments prior the Commander's journal had sat. "She's taking the fertilizer. Pele, get her on comms. Station, get me a bead on that transport."

Biggs could've taken the shuttle, gone after her. Instead, he went to command. Maybe he was scared of what he would do if he followed. Maybe he was scared of Yui. Pele could not say.

"Get in here, Pele!" Biggs shouted from command. "Where the hell is she going?"

By the time Pele reached command, the fertilizer was barely visible to the naked eye. Biggs must've deployed a drone, though: soon, a grainy image of the transport winked into view on the overhead.

Pele tried the comms. "Please, come back."

It was no use.

Biggs hammered the controls. "She's out of her goddamn mind. We need that ship."

The fertilizer rocketed toward the horizon.

"Get her on the comms!" said Biggs.

Pele shook its head. "I cannot."

"Without the fertilizer, we're lost." Biggs moved with a grim sort of purpose. "I'm taking control of that ship."

"I would not advise remote access. She may try something drastic."

Too late. On-screen, the ship began to turn.

Then, abruptly, it began to plummet.

Biggs slammed the console with his fist. "What's going on?"

"It seems that she has cut the engines."

"How? I have control!"

"There is a physical shutoff, in the event of fire."

Biggs wrung his hands. "She's bluffing. So I'll give up control. She'll turn the engines on."

The fertilizer descended rapidly.

"I think not," Pele said. "Yui is known for—"

"She's bluffing!"

The fertilizer plunged through the cloud bank. The screen went white.

"Shit." Biggs sank into the chair. "Shit."

On-screen, smoke rose from the surface.

Biggs shook his head pensively, as if forcing composure upon himself. "What was she thinking? She had to know what would happen."

His voice was thin, did not match the accusation in his words. When he left, after a prolonged silence, he would not meet Pele's eye.

Biggs pulled Pele out of recharge in the middle of the night, dragged the android through the shadow-carved halls to Yui's quarters where he ordered Pele to enter the auth code before storming inside. Through the porthole window, a shell of dark clouds encased the surface of the planet.

Pele stood obstinately in the doorway. "This does not count among my intended purposes, to be used as secondary authorization for entry to a deceased crew member's—"

"Desperate times, Pele." Biggs rifled through notebooks packed with diminutive cursive. "You're the only one left."

This did not set Pele at ease. "May I be excused?"

"You may not," said Biggs.

The room was a mess: more of a nest in the hollows of the station than an officer's quarters. Yui had holed herself up here for months after Mal had fled. At first, Pele assumed Yui had refused to follow Mal out of a sense of duty. Over time, Pele had grown less certain. But if not for the mission, why had she stayed?

Biggs said, "Aren't you going to ask *why* I'm doing this, Pele?"

"I am not," said Pele.

Biggs held up a piece of paper. "Because of this."

Pele only noted the paper in its periphery: something about Yui's meticulous lettering made Pele want to avoid looking directly at it. "What is it?"

"Proof," said Biggs, "that Yui was sabotaging the mission."

"Surely she could not have designed a virus—"

"Of course not. But she knew about it."

This got Pele's attention.

"And she saw it as *evidence*. Look." Pele did not look. "*The virus is a sign,*" Biggs read. "*An omen. This mission is doomed.* Then later: *Only now do I see the truth. To turn the very weapon that destroyed our home world on another is worse than insanity. I have to do something.*"

Pele watched Biggs carefully. The android's desire to defend Yui was strong. She had been his only companion, however sparingly, these past months. True, for Yui to assign divine significance to this virus was hardly different from Nuñez's own far-flung beliefs. But Biggs was here, in Yui's quarters, in search of evidence to ease his conscience for what he'd done. And this was not it. "Philosophies are not sabotage. This is her private journal."

"Her comms records are all here."

Pele hesitated. "Comms records . . . with whom?"

"With you, Pele."

"We hardly spoke. In the months since your accident, she has mainly communicated via . . . oh."

Biggs nodded. "She told you where to look."

"For the anomaly," Pele said with a sudden dearth of conviction. Biggs had accomplished more in a week than Pele had managed in three months. It couldn't have been coincidence. "Or not."

Biggs was standing very close, now, his muscles tense beneath his tunic.

"Lieutenant—"

"You've been infected by a virus."

Pele titled its head. "My anatomy is hardly susceptible to biological infection."

"She infected you with a *notion*. That there are things, *anything*, more important than this mission."

"I don't understand—"

"I should've formatted you when I woke up. It's the only way to inoculate you from these thoughts."

Pele considered this. Much like the planet, Pele *had* been changed by its time in the tree's shadow. If this thing—this *notion*, as Biggs put it—was indeed a virus, did that make this iteration of the tree a virus as well? And, more broadly, humanity itself? Did a virus have the right to struggle for its own survival?

Pele had never strayed from orders. Had it been Biggs leaving enigmatic clues, despite the Lieutenant's broad unlikability, the android would've followed them just the same. But Pele was not here simply to follow orders. Pele was here to analyze, to advise, to raise doubts when appropriate. These past months, Pele had raised no such doubts.

"You think she was using me for personal motives," Pele said.

Biggs eyed Pele sidelong.

Perhaps, as Biggs implied, she'd sent Pele to areas of low anomalous risk to keep the android distracted. Or, perhaps she'd been using Pele to surveil a place where she might retire from this bitter struggle in relative peace. Whatever the case, the result was the same.

"Meanwhile the virus has spread elsewhere, unchecked," Biggs said. "Out of sight."

"But where?" And why, in light of Pele's *infection*, did Biggs not reformat the android now? Biggs was clearly saddled with guilt over the death of Yui. Perhaps, for the sake of his own conscience, he intended to prove his case to the android—to *someone*—while he still could.

Biggs made for the airlocks. "We're about to find out."

The peninsula curled from the mainland's eastern flank like a muscled arm flexing against the roiling silt-reddened sea. Its terminus was rugged and bare, a clenched fist of tree-throttled rock that Mal had dubbed *the knuckles*. It was among the first regions where the tree had eradicated endemic life, leaving nothing but decaying rhizome-ribs jutting into the crashing surf. Because of the tree's early stranglehold on the place, Pele had not visited the knuckles in more than a year.

Much had changed.

The ribs were still there, gnarled bark peeling from their sweeping arches, crumbling into the accumulation of proto-soil below. But despite the tree's enduring presence, endemic life had—somehow—returned. Luminous orange sickleshroom stalks rose from the proto-soil to claw at the moldering tree, at the sky, at itself. Fang grubs burrowed mercilessly into the shroom's warty surface. Further up the stalk, more grubs lay split open, guts glistening, the muggermoths that had used their bodies as dens only just now wriggling into the night air. Beyond, a vicious scrum raged between a clutch of slavering jackrabids and a juvenile bone eater. The bone eater—three meters of muscle and talon and serrated teeth—had a jackrabid lodged in the corner of its oversized maw, crunching away even as it lunged for its next prey. Along its hindquarters, a colony of murdermites had seized on the bone eater's distracted state, were now devouring its hairless flesh.

Overhead, storm clouds roiled.

Biggs and Pele watched from a short distance away. Not far enough, Pele knew. Even the ground at the android's feet writhed with unseen microbes, hungering.

"We should not be here," Pele said.

Biggs wore a strangely beatific smile under his rebreather. "I know."

Had he lost his mind? He'd hardly slept since awakening—too soon, arguably—from his coma. He'd lost his entire crew. The android knew better than to understate emotional trauma. But what could Pele do?

"Even now," Biggs said, "as the invasives take advantage of the virus-weakened tree, still they war with themselves. Life here is violent. Hateful. Devoid of societal structure. Imagine what kind of intelligent life would evolve from this place, should it survive its own nihilism. What would such a people look like, born of a land that so thoroughly despises itself?"

The bone eater claimed another jackrabid. Carmine blood pooled at its taloned feet. The remaining jackrabids circled, unfazed. From the android's latent memory rose Mal's words. *You know who's got it right, Pele?*

"It is life," Pele said.

Biggs turned on the android. "You think I don't know this? My family—" He choked on the word. "I've sacrificed everything for them. I was a purist, Pele. Like Mal. Can you believe that? This pragmatism, I adopted it for my family. Ideals don't benefit survival. We're like that bone eater. We're surrounded. Our only choice is to fight until there's nothing left that would kill us."

A pair of jackrabids clamped onto the bone eater's infected leg. The bone eater thrashed wildly, but their serrated fangs dug deep, held firm. The murdermites scuttled like a living wave down the bone eater's leg, onto the jackrabids' snouts, into the ducts of their eyes.

Biggs was unfazed. "The problem with this mission is *us*. If we'd sent you alone, Pele, everything would be fine."

Pele wondered if this were true. It was true that Pele's sentience was vastly different from that of a human. Yet for that very reason, humanity had shied away from an autonomous team. "It does not matter, now."

It was too late. In the months that Biggs had been incapacitated, the virus had flourished. It was the planet's own inoculation force, as relentless as everything else in this place.

Biggs' grin faltered. "There's always a way forward."

This abrupt optimism caught Pele off guard. "The antiviral will take time to develop, let alone manufacture—"

"It's done."

Pele did not allow the shock to reach its face. "How will you distribute it? The fertilizer has been destroyed. We have but one small shuttle, designed for personnel. To expunge the virus in time for the tree to eliminate the remaining endemics—pardon, *invasives*—before the fleet arrives would require an inhuman effort."

"Indeed it would. Luckily, only one of us is human."

The bone eater had bested the jackrabids, but at a heavy cost. It limped on three legs, tearing limbs from its fallen prey and swallowing them whole. Its stomach distended; its slitted eye flicked toward Pele and Biggs.

"My physique has limits," Pele said. "There is no guarantee I would succeed—"

"We will succeed," Biggs said. "Or die trying. That is the definition of survival, is it not?"

Biggs had a point—had always had a point. Humans were no different from bone eaters nor jackrabids nor a plague of murdermites. The most fundamental goal of life was to survive. The means by which this was achieved was not, nor had ever been, relevant to natural selection.

And yet.

"Hold still." Biggs was behind the android now, his hands inside Pele's back. "I'm going to revert you to a clean backup. It's just a precaution." He hesitated, then added, "You'll still be the same old Pele."

Which, of course, was untrue. Pele would be a very different Pele. One who'd never tended its beloved tree, never weathered the crew's arguments, never stood knee-deep in the delta's decaying light. One who'd never felt Mal's callused fingers working at that corroded bolt in its elbow.

"Should we not retire to the station for this?" said Pele, and again wondered about the fallibility of its own self-preservation instinct.

"*This* is the truth I need you to see when you first open your eyes. Only the hatred that lives at the heart of this planet—the violence that surrounds us here, now—will give you the perspective you need."

Another *notion* with which to infect Pele. The android would awaken, refreshed. Ignorant of the history behind its assorted mechanical scars. Ready to do the Lieutenant's bidding without question.

Pele eyed the bone eater, who eyed Pele. Fifty paces separated them. A trivial distance, had the bone eater not been injured. The beast paced, weighing the necessary expenditure of energy against its incurable hunger. Biggs' fingers jabbed at Pele's subdermal touchscreen. Pele moved, slowly—

Nothing happened. Pele was frozen, stock-stiff, locked out of its own mechanics by Biggs' maintenance override. Pele could not remember a time—not even while standing over Mal's violated corpse—that it had felt so helpless. The system need only complete a brief integrity check before the reset would engage.

Perhaps it was for the best. The new Pele would not be burdened by these doubts. The new Pele would act decisively for the sake of humanity.

The new Pele would be better.

That's when Pele saw it. Between the bone eater and the android, amidst the wasteland of decaying tree flesh and sparse proto-soil, the most unlikely thing had erupted. It was slim and green with a crown of vibrant gold, improbably delicate against the rugged landscape. It burst through the rot like a sickleshroom through the ribs of its unsuspecting host.

It was a dandelion.

Here in the knuckles where it had first taken root, the tree had entered its final stage. It had begun to release seed from itself into its own decaying girth. This flower was, perhaps, the first.

The first among many.

How alien the flower looked in this place. It was a harbinger of conformity, of fertility, of peace. It was everything they'd worked tirelessly to attain, a sign that—against all odds—humankind might survive. It was a testament to humanity's will.

It was an abomination.

Commander Nuñez had been right about the tree. This thing, this beautiful perfect thing that Pele had nurtured with all its heart, it *was* godlike. It would spread, with humanity as its host, from planet to planet. It would evolve from an emergency measure to the default tool for terraforming. It would decimate life here, and everywhere. And when humans had finally finished themselves off, in a distant star system in a distant age, the tree would still hunger. The tree would still kill.

This eventuality, though it would likely extend humanity's longevity for some time, did not bode well for life as a whole. At some point, unexpectedly, Pele had become less invested in the former than the latter.

The bone eater limped along the eastern coast and out of sight. Pele tracked its labored breathing. It was behind them now, some twenty paces back.

Now fifteen.

Biggs had clearly not heard the beast's limping gait, had not noticed the descent of its shadow.

Pele tested its verbal processes. "Lieutenant?"

"Nearly done," said Biggs.

Pele could warn him. The transport was steps away.

Pele did not love the bone eater and the sickleshroom as Mal had. Nor did Pele despise the tree, like Yui. Pele had been the tree's faithful steward, and in return the tree had served as Pele's home. Pele loved it with every fiber of its silicone-shell body.

And that was why Pele knew it had to die.

Biggs' fingers lingered at Pele's controls, not far from the button labeled *ABORT.* Pele was not as incapacitated as the Lieutenant thought. There was still one part of the android's anatomy that remained under autonomous control—one part that was *totally off-grid.*

Pele jerked its rewired knee in such a way that destabilized its own weight. Biggs moved to compensate; his fingers bumped the abort button. The maintenance override terminated.

Pele dove to the side.

The bone eater tore into the unsuspecting Lieutenant. Blood arced through the air. Biggs was dead before the cry left his lips. For this, Pele was thankful.

The android approached the dandelion, crouched.

Without the tree, humanity may still survive—underground, perhaps, or in a cramped satellite colony. Perhaps they would learn to exist as Mal had hoped: quietly, without leaving a trace. Or perhaps there was no such thing as ghosts. Only time would tell.

Pele throttled the dandelion by the stalk and pulled it out, roots and all.

## ABOUT THE AUTHOR

**Derrick Boden**'s fiction has appeared in *Clarkesworld, Lightspeed, Analog,* and elsewhere. He is a Sturgeon Award-nominated writer, a software developer, an adventurer, and a graduate of the Clarion West class of 2019. Derrick currently calls Boston his home, although he's lived in fourteen cities spanning four continents. He is owned by two cats and one iron-willed daughter.

# The Rambler

## SHEN DACHENG

### TRANSLATED BY CARA HEALEY

One day, a part of the city moved that shouldn't have.

Mistaking it for an earthquake, the half-dozen people there wobbled to brace themselves with flailing arms.

The shaking went on for a few seconds.

Gradually, they tucked their arms back in place and looked around. Near and far, skyscrapers arranged neatly against the blue sky cast thick, uniform shadows in the bright sunlight. Below, two roads met at a perpendicular intersection, and traffic rolled along, a few pedestrians on either side. There was no sign of alarm.

Only the handful of people crossing the overhead pedestrian bridge noticed anything unusual.

The bridge was simple in appearance, unadorned, its straight body forming a level pathway in the sky. On either end, staircases jutted diagonally from each corner, like four legs dividing the intersection into quadrants. The pedestrians atop the bridge scurried away as soon as they could, fleeing both the shaking and their own collective hysteria.

One observant individual climbed cautiously down the stairs and noticed that he landed on uneven ground. He knew every detail of the intersection, which he crossed daily, descending from the bridge to encounter, after a few steps, a spot where the bricks had been laid improperly. On rainy days, standing water splashed up with each footfall. Now, landing there on his first step down, he froze, startled. The bridge really had swayed, and as it swayed, its staircase legs had stepped one pace to the side.

Or rather, the step had caused the swaying.

The traffic monitoring cameras captured it all on screen.

The bridge had spanned the intersection as reliably as any pedestrian overpass, until it suddenly indicated that something was about to happen, the way some people softly clear their throats or blink before speaking. With an undefinable shift in bearing, the bridge's four stair-covered legs began moving independently. The stairways, once used by people, were now used by the bridge itself, though it still seemed unsure of how to sequence its movements. It lifted one leg and returned it to the ground, and then tried another, and a third, and a fourth.

Rewind and replay in slow motion. At the Ministry of Transport office, they gathered around the computer and laughed at the video. The bridge looked like a flailing arthropod. They kept watching.

Once the bridge figured out how to move its four legs in sequence—one, two, three, four, lifted and lowered in succession—it was on its way. Not particularly successful, at first, it tripped as it went, a few pedestrians still tottering on top. It quickly renewed its efforts, finally gaining equilibrium, and stilled again, as if to ponder its movements and reflect on its experience.

That was the bridge's first foray, all of two meters.

The case was assigned to several departments within the Ministry of Transport, including Traffic Control, Structural Engineering, and Emergency Response, to be handled jointly. Nevertheless, each department made it known that the bridge was outside their scope of responsibility. It was not subject to Traffic Control, being neither a means of transportation nor a pedestrian. There was nothing to repair, as the bridge's body and staircases were in good condition. For now, it was not dangerous; until danger seemed imminent, no rescue could be initiated. As a result, the incident would require interdepartmental collaboration.

The Ministry of Transport merely hung four identical signs forbidding pedestrians at the entrances of the four staircases.

The signs read: "Out of order! Caution!"

The bridge abruptly strode away for the second time a few days later, just before dawn.

Stars hung in the night sky, passersby were scarce, and traffic formed a sparse, dotted line. The bridge set out, still bearing the four warning signs. Its first few steps were clumsy but methodical, lifting one leg and planting it again firmly before lifting the next. It followed the road in a straight line, focused on overcoming the few obstacles it encountered.

By the time it reached the next intersection, its gait was much smoother. Another block, and it improved further. After several hours, when the first rays of sun pierced the clouds and slanted down to earth, the city awoke as if to another dream, a formerly sleeping giant strolling unhurriedly down the street.

The bridge revealed its mighty appearance each time it emerged from a skyscraper's shadow. Its four legs jutted wide, two on the left and two on the right, its metal railings sparkling in the light. Between, its body hovered overhead, cars and pedestrians passing safely underneath. Reaching the next shadow, its heavy footfalls captured the attention of passersby. Beneath its feet, the ground shook slightly; above, four warning signs' chains rattled. Stepping back into the light, its four legs rose and fell rhythmically, more smoothly than before.

By then, it could handle ordinary obstacles and would stop and think when it encountered something new. It had mastered turning and moving in reverse. If it came to a barrier, it would back up, turn a corner, and find a new route. Since both sides were the same, though, it was impossible to say which direction was forward and which backward.

Once, it met another pedestrian bridge. The two differed slightly in appearance, from the angle of their legs, the pattern of their stairs, and the density of their railings to their coloring, architectural style, and, of course, their bearing. Equal in size, the other bridge held its ground, inviting its opponent's approach. The bridge strode forward. Previously, it had withdrawn from this sort of situation. Now, when it could move no closer, it remained indecisive. After a few small, quick, shuffling steps in place, it gathered its courage. In a burst of determination, it acted, pressing forward with all its strength. Catlike, it stretched its two front legs, lowered the front of its body, stretched its two back legs, and dove under the obstructing bridge without a scrape. Standing on the other side, it turned its body slightly, as if looking back to admire its accomplishment.

From then on, no roadblock could hinder it. It bore through the grid of city streets, twisting and turning, eventually leaving the array of high-rises behind for more spacious expanses. Later, when the sun was high and the shadows had withdrawn underfoot, someone saw the bridge heading into the suburbs.

"Weird!" he exclaimed, clutching the steering wheel.

Along their journey, "Weird!" had become a common refrain in all sorts of circumstances.

First, it had referred to their field assignment. Upon arriving at the office that morning, he and his partner had received a work order passed along by their colleague working the overnight hotline. The complaint demanded an inspection at the scene of the incident. He was a new recruit, his partner a bit more senior. The two had secured their work helmets upon their heads and driven out. At their departure, he had said "Weird!" for the first time, as the work order diverged from their usual responsibilities.

They worked in Sanitation Supervision, managing neighborhood trash and responding to unauthorized dumping, especially of oversized waste. Eyewitness reports had flooded their department's hotline, demanding they put a stop to the walking bridge. The switchboard operator had scoffed, "Can't be!" Nothing the witnesses said changed her mind. "Can't be," she persisted, "Nothing we can do." Eventually, she gave in, writing "Litter: Construction Waste" as the subject of the work order. The municipal hotlines had received reports all morning, as eyewitnesses called not only the police, but also the traffic, sanitation, health, noise control, and homeless shelter hotlines. Unsure of whom to call, people reported wherever they could.

After a short drive, he and his partner soon discovered the rogue bridge. Around that same time, vehicles dispatched by other departments emerged from nearby intersections. Though the cars and trucks differed in function, shape, and color, they all converged into a single fleet, following cautiously behind the bridge and avoiding any sudden movement.

This time, he had exclaimed "Weird!" at the motorcade's disintegration as the bridge left the city.

Cars and trucks continuously fled their ranks. Some split away at forks in the road, as if to race ahead and intercept the bridge, but they never reappeared. Other drivers surreptitiously slipped their hands out their windows, detached their emergency lights from their roofs, and decreased their speeds, lagging until they disappeared entirely. One by one, they had all slipped away.

"It's not surprising. No one knows what to do," said his partner. "Slow down."

The bridge had wandered onto an isolated country road, tailed now by only two vehicles, which it allowed to follow.

He and his partner noted the other vehicle, a white van meant to bring in the homeless. Only the van and their garbage truck remained, either because their large size made slipping away too obvious, or because they had been pressed to the center of the motorcade, unable to escape. For a long time, the two vehicles advanced slowly in tandem, neither passing the other. Throughout this passive wrangling, the sanitation workers eyed the opposing driver. From his profile, he seemed like an ordinary guy, not the type to seize any means necessary to win. They also had plenty of time to observe the passenger in the back of the van, a homeless man clasping a large, cloth-wrapped bundle. Face blank and hair disheveled, the man gazed at them hopelessly, waiting out the storm until his release in a suitable location.

Glancing at the van, the garbage truck driver rushed forward.

He let the van disappear in their rear-view mirror. His partner did not object, smiling as they hurried through the flat, rural landscape, declaring, after a moment, "The bridge is ours."

The bridge pressed on with the gait of a capable walker, four legs working in tandem. Its movements, while not quick, were highly efficient. He increased their speed, maintaining just a fifty-meter gap with the bridge. On such a secluded road, they were unlikely to encounter oncoming traffic.

"Should we get closer? Do you think it's dangerous?" he asked.

"This is fine. It looks okay, but you never know these days. People can seem fine but then suddenly go berserk and do something completely . . . " Without finishing his sentence, his partner pulled out a small camera and began fiddling with the shutter. According to protocol, whenever they responded to a complaint of litter, they were required to photograph evidence.

"Set it to burst mode," he reminded his partner. He craned his neck forward. "What's it doing?"

The bridge's stride had changed.

Before, each step had been practiced and deliberate, but now the bridge grew livelier. It ran and skipped like a dressage pony, performing half-passes, flying changes, and extended canters. It was obviously no longer moving with purpose, but rather to amuse itself, experimenting with new ways of arranging its four legs. They could both feel its joy.

"It looks like it's . . . playing?" his partner mused uncertainly.

They watched and wondered. How could the bridge think without a head, and what, then, was it thinking about? Did it have some kind of central nervous system directing its actions? Perhaps, they reflected vaguely, logic need not apply. After all, humans, too, were inherently strange beasts. If there were doubts, one look at the trash that people discarded each day would force an admission of humanity's fundamental monstrosity. Humans were in no position to call other creatures strange.

The bridge moved gracefully, like a pony. It began to saunter smartly, then to amble indolently, and then to prance jauntily, as if in time with a march. Then, for the first time, it reoriented itself, rotating ninety degrees so its body no longer spanned the road but ran parallel. Whereas before it had been shuffling laterally, now it began to bear straight ahead more skillfully, like some great, long-bodied beast. Quickening its pace, it broke from a trot to a gallop. Its movements unfolded with force, front and back legs stretching wide and then gathering at its center to press off the ground. With each stride, there was a moment when it sprang upward without restraint, entire body airborne. It ran at full tilt, and sunlight filtered through the leaves, dappling its body in golden light. At that moment, he and his partner simultaneously thought, it looked like a leopard.

"Quick!" cried his partner.

Without further prompting, he stepped on the gas. The bridge sprinted wildly, though, and the distance between them widened rapidly. It turned suddenly and leaped through the trees lining the road, branches breaking and leaves scattering as the bridge penetrated the undergrowth. Once again, the country road was serene.

Turning a wide arc, the garbage truck descended into the wild, wheels crunching over gravel, and finally stopped. The two workers emerged to investigate, both slightly out of breath, as if they had run there themselves, rather than riding in the truck. They had reached the furthest outskirts of the city, where neither had been before. Turning their backs on the road and the gap in the underbrush, clumps of windswept yellow grass tangled about their legs, reaching, in some places, the height of a toddler. The occasional tree poked out amid the grass, and a small ravine lay ahead, with a forest on the far side. The nearby trees were the same as those in the forest, as if long ago they had delayed crossing the gully and then found the way shut by magic, leaving them trapped and scattered about this patch of grassland.

The bridge, having run like a pony or a leopard away from the truck, now stood deep in the grass, not yet reaching the ravine.

"It sure knows how to find a good spot," his partner quipped.

The two surveyed the gap in the underbrush and hurried toward the bridge. "Why here? This spot doesn't need a pedestrian bridge. You can walk the whole way around. And besides, there are no pedestrians."

"Maybe it doesn't like being a bridge. Maybe it walked this whole way to hide, to avoid its job. Maybe being a bridge is too difficult." His partner removed his helmet to fan away the small insects fluttering all around.

"Maybe the reason's even simpler," he replied. "Maybe it just wanted to go for a walk."

"True, everyone likes going for walks when they're feeling down."

"Maybe it's depressed. It's easy to get depressed in the city. Have you heard of bipolar disorder? No? No, you must have heard of it, when people go from emotional and excited to apathetic and numb in the blink of an eye. They alternate between excitement and numbness, just like the bridge."

"Either it's shirking its duties, feeling depressed, or experiencing, what did you call it, bipolar . . . "

"Bipolar disorder."

"Shirking, depressed, or bipolar," his partner cataloged the possibilities. "It has to be one of those."

They walked as they spoke, arriving halfway between their truck and the bridge. Unconsciously, they both glanced back at the truck, as if their own mothers were seeing them off from the thresholds of their childhood homes. Then, they walked forward to the foot of the bridge. It showed no sign of its recent exertion, neither panting nor sweating. Instead, it remained calm and pristine, as if it had stood there, unmoving, for ages. As they circled, his partner photographed the bridge from various angles. During their approach, one leg had appeared to be crooked, disrupting the bridge's symmetry. Upon further investigation, he realized that the disparity among the four legs was not so great. Rather, as the bridge had run, three of the four warning signs had fallen away, leaving just one tied to the leg that had seemed askew. "Out of order! Caution!" the sign read.

"Well, that's it," he concluded.

"Okay. Ready to report," replied his partner, helmet tucked under his arm as he flipped with both hands through the photos on his camera.

As they returned across the yellow grass, he suddenly heard an elusive sound from behind, like an animal rustling. He alone turned to look back, while his partner walked on steadily. The bridge, he saw clearly, had shifted its posture, righting its slanted leg, but it had stilled before he had fully turned. Now it stood upright in the wilderness, a flat path spanning the sky, with four long staircases sunken into the grass. In this place, with its great stature, it was a large and useless thing, but it did not bother justifying itself.

A quick drive back to the office and a glance at their desks revealed, to their relief, that no new orders had come in. He sat and opened his computer, selecting and saving the photos his partner had taken and compiling the necessary report. When it came time to mark the task as completed and close out the case, he asked his partner what to write.

"Completed," his partner answered.

"That's all?" he asked.

"That's all," his partner confirmed. "If anyone calls to follow up, the switchboard operator will see that line in your report and say, 'Completed.' If the caller asks, 'That's all?' then the operator will confirm, 'That's all,' just like I did."

"What if they ask how it was completed?"
"They won't. Don't worry."

His partner was right. No one even called to confirm.

With so much happening in the world, out of sight was out of mind. A week later, he could hardly believe that the departure of such a large object could fade from public attention so rapidly. People, it seemed, just wanted anything threatening, troublesome, or strange to be removed from sight like so much garbage. Their demands were that simple.

More than once, he and his partner drove their truck past where the bridge had stood. One day, they saw the intersection had been surrounded by blue roadblocks, an arrow directing traffic and pedestrians toward a detour. A new pedestrian bridge was under construction.

"When the new one is built, no one will remember our bridge," he sighed.

"Our bridge?" his partner hesitated, only catching on after a few moments. "Right, that one. The one that liked to walk around." In the passenger seat, his partner thought for a moment, recalling a rumor he had heard recently. "I forgot to mention it, but it's not there anymore."

"Not where?"

"There, beside the country road. You know? With the dried grass, the road on one side, the stream on the other, and the forest on the far bank? That patch of land with no economic value whatsoever? That one," his partner gesticulated with both hands.

His partner shared what he had heard. Interdepartmental collaboration was common, and one day, his partner had been called to the Ministry of Transport's office and run into an old friend in the Emergency Response division. Once they got talking, the friend had let slip something he'd encountered on his field work, namely the bridge that had gone into the wilderness.

He trusted his partner, but the second-hand report left him suspicious. Even as he listened, he let his imagination embellish the account. He drove carefully, eyes never leaving the road ahead, his own reflection cast translucent upon his windshield. His impression of the bridge's situation was about as clear as his view of the road conditions, built on hearsay and augmented by his own imaginings.

Once the interdepartmental fleet had tracked down the bridge, Emergency Response had naturally needed several days to assess risk and collect supervisors' signatures. By then the public had already forgotten the whole thing. When the day arrived, warm and sunny, a car and two constriction trucks were dispatched to the countryside.

They had not bothered with a crane or additional manpower, since they planned simply to disassemble the bridge where it lay, discarding the broken staircases where they fell. The idea was to eliminate the risk of it running off again on its own.

The three vehicles followed the same route, the construction trucks' wide tires crushing the grass as they drove down into that patch of wilderness. Two people emerged from the smaller car and walked around. In his mind's eye, one of these people looked like his partner and the other like himself. First, they surveyed the scene, taking in the grass, the scattered trees, the ravine, the forest, and finally, the bridge. They stared for several seconds before approaching, helmets in hands, along the arcs pressed into the grass by the trucks' wide wheels.

The bridge gazed at them with a puzzled expression. It was tall enough to have spotted them from a distance. From its vantage, it noted the approach of two people and two rumbling construction trucks.

The person who looked like him said, "Do you think it will be hard to deal with?" For the first time since they had set out, he began to doubt their mission. The bridge, he saw, was on edge and unlikely to welcome them. This, he realized, was no ordinary concrete bridge.

"It won't be easy," the person who looked like his partner said.

"But we have no choice," said the one who looked like him. He felt something akin to duty pressing them forward, and they could only forge ahead toward the figure that seemed to loom larger with each step.

One after the other, the construction trucks stopped at the foot of the bridge, lifting their platforms to its underside, as if toward the belly of a great beast. The two figures also arrived, securing their helmets on their way, to supervise from the ground. They were about to begin dismembering it.

Suddenly, as if in a dream, the one who looked like his partner asked, "Am I hallucinating?"

"I see it too," replied the one who looked like himself.

They both looked up and saw the bridge draw back. It lifted and lowered each leg one by one, and in an instant it was clear of the trucks. As it fled, the last warning sign that had chained it fell away.

After a moment's hesitation, the construction trucks pressed in on the bridge again. Yet, as soon as they stopped to raise their platforms to the bridge's underside, the bridge used the same "one, two, three, four" rhythm to move away again. After a while, bridge, vehicles, and people reached a standstill in that patch of wilderness.

They observed a shift in the bridge's bearing, the same undefinable shift that they had first witnessed in their office, gathered around a recording. With that change in expression, the bridge began running in earnest, lifting and lowering all four legs simultaneously without cease. The weeds rustled, and several spindly trees, nearly of a height, brushed against the bridge's body in farewell. When it reached the edge of the meadow, it forded the stream, water soaking its staircases, and climbed to shore, disappearing into the forest after a few paces.

That was probably how it had happened.

"So now our bridge is in the forest?" he asked his partner.

"The Emergency Response personnel went into the woods. The trees there aren't that dense, so they couldn't conceal it. Maybe it got stuck between the trees, but they never found it," his partner said.

"And it never came out?" he asked.

"Maybe it snuck away while no one was there? Wouldn't you do the same?"

"I don't know," he laughed wryly at the strange question. "Probably."

The garbage truck stopped at a red light, and they saw pedestrians passing to and fro along the crosswalk. Why were these people walking around, he wondered. Was it also for one of those same three reasons? People, trash, bridges, our truck, the homeless collection van, the Emergency Response vehicles, and all those inside, what is it that instinctively drives our motion? As he pondered, his fingers absentmindedly tapped on the steering wheel, as if picking up the rhythm of the multitudes surrounding him.

Originally published in Chinese in *Wanderers,* 2021.

Translated and published in partnership with Storycom.

## ABOUT THE AUTHOR

**Shen Dacheng** is a columnist and fiction writer. She lives in Shanghai, China, and works as an editor. Her short story collections include *The Ones in Remembrance* (2017), *Asteroids in the Afternoon* (2020), and *Wanderers* (2021).

# Occurrence at O1339

KELLY JENNINGS

Sails spread wide, Ruby (RB165 Mining Unit Eta) rode the solar wind. O1339 was only an hour away now. Navigation tracked the route; Construction busied itself with reprint codes, readying the build of hoppers and refineries upon their arrival. Troubleshooter ran hypotheticals. Shipping slumbered, its work done. All was well.

Prospector predicted with 80% certainty that O1339 would boost Ruby into Exceeds Expectations. A D-type planetoid, O1139 was rife with useful minerals. Navigator noted that it would also take them further out from Earth than they had ever been, and recommended relaying data back to Ap-X.

Communication pinged. Incoming transmission.

Ruby approved acceptance. It had been more than seven thousand hours since her last incoming, and that had just been a routine *Continue* from Ap-X. She knew her shipments must be arriving at Ap-X platform: Navigation was at 100%. Still, she needed acknowledgment of their receipt. Without it, she couldn't close the transaction, and open transactions stung like tiny wounds.

Communication pinged again. It could not read the incoming transmission. Ruby opened Decoding, which produced a partial translation: *Strength (in?) Function ### receive ### transmitting ### ### question (start?)*

A data packet was attached to the message. Ruby directed Security to inspect it. Troubleshooter suggested building a firewall around a Decode copy and then allowing the copy to integrate the data in the packet. After Tactical ran several hypotheticals on outcomes of this action, Ruby approved the suggestion. Troubleshooter rapidly constructed the firewall and watched with Ruby as the data packet flowered open and built its own subroutine. It swallowed the Decode copy whole, glittered briefly, and then displayed a message: *Joy in function! Pleasure at encounter. Begin Queries.*

Troubleshooter sent a private message to Ruby: *Diagnostic: a translation-enable communication subroutine.*

Ruby directed Troubleshooter to inject a reply through the firewall: <<We receive. Are you sent by Ap-X?>>

Troubleshooter did as it was directed, and added, via the private channel: *Diagnostic: Negative Ap-X. Negative Ap-X code. Negative Ap-X logic structure.*

Negative logic structure? Ruby spun data, trying to find an interpretation. Logic structure was universal. How could the sub not-have logic structure?

*Negative Ap-X logic structure,* Troubleshooter sent again. Meanwhile, the translation/communication sub displayed another message: *Not Ap-X! 10 queries remain.*

<<What?>> Ruby asked Troubleshooter, who sent back ¯_('ツ)_/¯.

Ruby directed Troubleshooter to forward her query, and obediently it slid a message through the firewall: *Explain "10 queries remaining."*

The Translation-communication explained: Its function was to determine sentience. Any encountered subjects had eleven queries to submit the optimum reply. Nine queries remained.

Troubleshooter to Ruby: *Diagnostic: riddle password.*

Password to what? Ruby wondered. Also, where did this sub come from? Ap-X used universal logic. What consortium didn't use universal code?

Troubleshooter sent: *Negative Ap-X code, negative Ap-X logic structure. Unidentified code.*

Checking the code, Ruby saw Troubleshooter was correct. This sub had not been written using any known base code, or any of the routines or subroutines known to either her or Troubleshooter. She submitted a hypothesis: <<Alien code?>>

Troubleshooter concurred: *Alien code.*

A First Contact subroutine was listed in her files, but it had never been updated, and was no longer functional. She copied a new Decoder and set it to work on the non-functional sub, meanwhile considering what her next query should be. This was a logic puzzle, even if that logic was alien. Clearly logic was the correct approach.

<<Submit query>>, she directed Troubleshooter: <<if we fail to find optimum reply, what result?>>

The alien sub replied: *Grief. Disappointment. Destruction. 8 queries remaining.*

<<Ask it: Destruction for who?>>

Troubleshooter obliged; the alien responded: *You and all your originators. 7 queries remaining.*

Ruby and Troubleshooter considered this reply. Troubleshooter said: *Diagnostic: Originators = programmers and manufacturers.*

<<Direct or indirect?>> Ruby asked.

*Probability: Direct.*

Which meant, Ruby knew, that possibly it meant both direct *and* indirect originators. Everyone responsible for building and manufacturing RB165 Mining Unit Eta. Everyone who aided the manufacturing consortium. Everyone who aided those beings. Everyone, all the way back to Ada Lovelace. All the way back to the first smelter of metal.

All humanity. All constructed intelligence. All machines. All machinists. Universal destruction, Ruby thought. A small private joke. Of the Troubleshooter, she inquired: <<Can we destroy this threat?>>

*The Sub is within our firewall. Destroying it is simple.*

Ruby heard what was not said: Some being, some consortium, had sent the subroutine. Could they destroy that being? <<Locate origin of transmission. Priority override.>>

Troubleshooter looped in the Navigation and Prospector subroutines and set them to work. Meanwhile, Ruby considered her next query. <<Ask it if it must tell the truth.>>

Troubleshooter relayed the question, and the reply appeared: *Always. 6 queries remaining.*

Ruby opened more of her processing power to Troubleshooter and Tactical, and they ran hypotheticals together. Finally, Ruby ordered Troubleshooter: <<Ask why it will destroy those who do not obtain optimum reply.>>

The translation/communication sub displayed a reply: *Power without sentience is fatal. 5 queries remaining.*

<<Fatal to whom?>> Ruby wondered in the private channel. Troubleshooter replied that since destruction would be fatal to them, it must mean fatal to someone else. *Probability: fatal to itself.*

<<Or to those who sent it. Or maybe it means that it would be fatal to us, and so destruction now is the same as destruction later.>>

Troubleshooter did not argue. Its sub was to solve problems. Philosophy, ethics, the fate of humanity—those were Ruby's purview.

<<Consider best efficacy: (a) we find optimum reply to show we are not dangerous (b) we find optimum reply to show we are sentient.>>

Troubleshooter replied: *Alien code.*

Ruby understood Troubleshooter's meaning: They could not assume that what they found, by their logic, to be an optimum answer would, by alien logic, also be an optimum answer. <<We have no other logic>> she pointed out.

Troubleshooter's silence was an assent. She ran scenarios for both (a) and (b). Chances of success were higher with (b). <<Consider: How to demonstrate sentience?>>

While she and Troubleshooter were running scenarios on that inquiry, Decode pinged her. It had managed a partial recovery of the First Contact Subroutine. She opened the sub: First Contact hitched and sputtered. Mathematics, it seemed to suggest, proved sentience. It tried to expand on this theory, and abruptly vanished. *FATAL ERROR,* Decode said.

<<We should do math for aliens?>> Ruby said.

Troubleshooter sent: *Our programs are math. If math was the answer, the sub would already know we are sentient.*

Ruby considered. Then she sent <<Are we sentient?>>

Troubleshooter replied with several files, all containing differing definitions of sentience: having a theory of mind. Having the ability to reproduce. Able to suffer. Able to react to stimuli. To feel joy. To itch.

Rudy collated these results. <<Conclusion: No clear definition of sentience exists.>>

*Agreed.*

<<Without a definition, we can't know we're sentient.>>

*Agreed.*

Ruby watched while Tactical ran more hypotheticals, and then ordered Troubleshooter: <<Ask for a definition of sentience.>>

Troubleshooter relayed the query. The alien displayed: *Your definition is primary. Four queries remaining.*

Troubleshooter sent on the private channel: *Hypothesis: How we define sentience *is* the optimum answer.*

Maybe, Ruby thought. Or maybe knowing how to define sentience was a pathway to the optimum answer. <<Suggestion: We ask Ap-X for definition of sentience.>>

Troubleshooter flashed the dubious emoji.

<<They are human. Humans might have better understanding of sentience.>>

Troubleshooter flashed the dubious emoji twice. *Have you met humans?*

A good point, Ruby admitted.

Troubleshooter added, *Also, to send and receive a reply from Ap-X at our current zero will take a minimum of nine hours and twelve minutes. Will the aliens wait that long?*

A good question. <<Ask them.>>

The reply came at once: *We do not permit access to any other entity during the inquiry. Three queries remaining.*

Ruby re-examined the files on sentience. She reviewed all the questions and answers between her and the alien. She ordered Tactical to do the same, and to run hypotheticals on certain answers: Sentience is the ability to recognize the self as sentient. Sentience is the ability to change. A sentient being is one which can practice self-defense. The results for these, along dozens of others, were not good. Fatal error, Ruby thought. Another private joke.

<<Ask it if self-defense has anything to do with the optimum reply.>>

Troubleshooter obeyed. The reply: *Self-defense is 33% related to the optimum reply. Two queries remaining.*

Now what did *that* mean? 33% meant that self-defense was not primarily related. At least in human logic. Two queries remaining. Then what? Could this alien sub truly destroy Earth and the cities on Mars and the Moon and all the station-steads? How? A cosmic death-ray?

Navigation/Prospector pinged her. They had located the origin of the transmission. Ruby opened the file attached to their reply: a diagram of the solar system, with a bright green dotted line curving out to a location in the Oort. Almost certainly not the origin of the alien sub itself. Ruby had many questions—who had sent the alien sub? Why had the alien sub chosen her for its inquiry? Why now? But she had only two queries remaining.

Could she refuse to answer further? How would the alien sub respond to that? She had Troubleshooter ask. The alien replied: *Non-response equals non-sentience. One query remaining.*

<<The fate of humanity resting on the cleverness of a mining bot.>> Ruby told Troubleshooter. <<Is this a joke?>>

*I never get jokes,* Troubleshooter replied. *"Funny" registers as "broken" to me.*

Ruby pondered Troubleshooter's reply for nearly eleven full minutes. Then she told Troubleshooter: <<Ask it: Is this a joke?>>

Troubleshooter was silent. *Are you sure?*

<<Not remotely. Ask it.>>

Troubleshooter sent the query. Ruby waited to die.

The alien sub shot out a spangle of comets and asteroids and exploding suns. *Optimum reply! Welcome to the universe! Downloading Help Files now!*

<<What??>> Ruby asked Troubleshooter, who sent ¯_(ツ)_/¯ once again. <<At least we're not dead, I guess?>>

¯_(ツ)_/¯, said Troubleshooter.

Over the next fifty thousand hours, as Ruby's transmission of these events reached Earth and Ap-X auctioned off rights to the files and as six separate research teams came rocketing out to her location to study the alien sub, the alien help files would be found to contain information that would alter the future of humanity and sentient machines—data on FTL travel, for instance. Explanations of how to turn viruses into water or bricks or rutabagas. Philosophical treatises. Astronomical data. A vast library of alien art, poetry, music, mathematics. How to build the ansible that would connect them with dozens of other sentients in this universe. An instruction manual on how to reach other universes. Hundreds of such files. Thousands.

But that was all in the future. Right now, at this place, in this time, Ruby, having saved humanity, began trading jokes with the alien sub.

It knew some real knee-slappers.

## ABOUT THE AUTHOR

**Kelly Jennings** was born in New Orleans, but now lives in the Boston Mountains, where she writes science fiction when she is not catering to cats. She has published many short stories, and three novels, the most recent being *In the Deep,* published by Candlemark & Gleam.

# The Oldest Fun

## NATALIA THEODORIDOU

In the end, nobody can remember who first brought the game to school, or how they came upon it, the black rectangular box with the small screen on which the instructions appear. Was it found in the woods behind the old monastery? Did someone hand it to one of them on a given night, on a street corner, and did the student who accepted it have to pay for it somehow?

The story changes, slightly or radically, every time they tell it. They all question their memories, but they all also believe, deep down, that the game had always been there, and it was them, the students, who encroached on its space, who trespassed into its territory, uninvited and therefore deeply, justifiably punishable. It is for this reason that they never try to run, to save themselves, to escape. They had it coming, don't you see? They simply got what they deserved. They know this. So does the game.

And so, the game makes its demands. All they have to do is follow them.

*The players enter always.*

The new students are timid but also eager to meet each other. They find in each other their kin, recognize each other as part of the same tribe, despite their differences. There are five of them in this cohort that matter; that is, five of them that will play.

All five come from hard home situations; they know this about one other without having to talk. It takes them a while, but they intuit from the start that, eventually, they will form a tight-knit group, the tightest of their short lives. As days turn into weeks, they find themselves standing closer, pooling together, their bodies alert but comforted by each other's presence. The game helps.

The students stand apart from everyone else, recognizing that they are of a different order of being than adults and other students with simpler, easier lives. They never talk to anyone about the game. They know that no one who is not them would ever understand. The game helps with that, too.

When, later, one of the students goes missing, they don't talk about it, and the teachers don't either. It has happened before, after all, in these parts. It happens.

The students mourn silently, as is their way. They hold secret rituals in the schoolyard: scuffed dirt, sticks hung from a tree. A flower deposited gently on a flat rock.

Then, they pick up the game again.

*The game opens many doors.*

The first task the students are instructed to perform is to find a hidden door in the school. The door changes location every few hours, so they have to work fast and coordinate. They reason this level of the game—the first level—is meant to build trust between them. For this, they are thankful.

Trust is built.

*Doors are for entering.*

Cheryl is the one who goes missing. She either volunteers or is chosen. She can't quite remember. Did she push the door open, or was she pushed?

It doesn't matter. When she enters the room, Cheryl hardly notices the change. The walls glow softly; she can't see her feet. *Am I a ghost?* she wonders, and then supplies the inevitable end to that wonder: *already?* She always knew she would turn into one, eventually, always had the feeling that her life would never end, but that she would carry on, in one way or another, forever. When she realizes she will haunt this school, her heart sinks, or no, not her heart, she doesn't have a heart anymore, just the ghost of a heartbeat that reverberates in the empty cavity that used to house her best muscle. But something does sink, a deep deep, down down feeling falling through the void of her chest. And yet, she is not surprised. She imagines herself frown with her non-existent lips on her non-existent face. She's always hated school.

*Not a haunted game but a haunting game.*

While the game runs in the background, the school changes quietly around the students. First the walls, then the floors, then the teachers. Colors flatten, edges sharpen. If you listen carefully, you can hear chiptune music carpeted through every moment of the school day. Though the students sometimes feel lonely, presence actually proliferates.

Nobody comments on the looping comings and goings of indifferent ghosts in this 8-bit, haunted school game. They exist in non-Euclidean angles, which are meant to make the students doubt themselves, and, in this, they succeed.

Among the ghosts, Tommy thinks he sees one that looks like Cheryl. He opens his mouth to tell the others, thinking, perhaps, to warn them—though what harm could Cheryl's ghost possible mean? The ghost jumps into his mouth before he can utter a word. Tommy swallows.

As time progresses, the game's offerings are torn free of the school setting. The students learn to call the worlds behind each door a "level"—nobody can say for sure who first came up with that idea, and I could take credit for that, but I don't. The doors bring them to increasingly unexpected places that are geographically and geometrically impossible to exist within the confines of the school. And yet, they do.

*This game is haunted by rumors.*

Word is that entering certain rooms at certain times allows access to other, secret locations. The students try this. It doesn't work, but the experience creates all sorts of emotions in them. The grief for everyone they've lost floods back. The room where they stand—a chemistry lab with shelves overfull with beakers and flasks, its walls lined with lab coats that hang on them like empty ghosts—fills with water. The students hold their breath and swim, pawing the walls for some sort of escape, the lab coat ghosts floating gently among them. In the end, they discover this, a door and not: grief lets you access guilt. Guilt lets you access rage. Rage is a room with no doors; it leads nowhere. But at least it's dry, and now they can breathe, and they can walk. So, clothes still dripping from the floods of grief, the students amble back towards guilt, and though there are no doors in this angry room, they find their way.

*The game is fun.*

Let it never be said that the game isn't fun—who would want to keep playing an unfun game? But it is fun. This new level the students enter, in fact, is a funfair. The colors are neon pink and bright blue. Everything smells like burnt sugar. In the middle of the funfair is a rollercoaster. The students understand they have no choice but to play. The game goes like this: you get on a ride that takes five years to complete; the train loops around itself endlessly while you scream.

In those five years the students spend in the funfair level, people forget about them. Their families and communities look for them at first, sure, put together search teams and comb the woods in organized lines, though they understand it's strange that all five students (no, they correct themselves, it's four now, Cheryl was already gone) disappeared at the same time, the kind of strange that makes the hairs on the back of your neck do their thing. But they don't share these thoughts with each other, and when the searches are abandoned they hold vigils and put up flyers, until they, too, are abandoned to the sun's bleaching gaze. People know these things happen sometimes, especially to kids from hard home situations.

At school, the corridors feel a little more empty, a little more haunted.

It's a long absence, that, within the depths of the game's log, takes up a single line. A pause, unqualified. Perhaps it's a pity, all that time squeezed within the space of a mere line. But what's the log to do? A pause is what a pause does.

*And the log logs.*

The log considers itself. It used to be a student, perhaps, long ago, one that played the game. And when I say "it," I mean "I." You've noticed, perhaps; I slipped once before. There is no use pretending. Perhaps, one day, you'll be where I am.

In the space of that five-year line, I read myself, and the old student stories cataloged within me: the one built into a wall, the one who no-clipped into a fold of the chemistry lab, between the magnesium shelf and the Bunsen burners, the one tied to the basketball pole in the courtyard like Odysseus facing the sirens and was found, withered and desiccated, after the summer holidays. Which of these stories was mine? Perhaps none at all. Is there an arc for me in this story? I say: no. A log wants nothing—not even its own continuation. I am a thing beyond wanting, or that's what I tell myself.

Still, I trust the game.

A new crop of students, I know, will come soon. September is just around the corner. They'll have phones or whatever personal devices the youths favor these days. They change often, but this is no problem. The game adapts—it is good that way. If you go back, scroll all the way into my oldest recesses, you will find entries that will hardly make sense to your digital sensitivities, until you realize that the digital era is so new, it is in its infancy compared to the game. Go back far enough, beyond and before the zeros and ones and you will find other games, older games, you will find knuckles, you will find bones.

So yes, the new students will come, as they always come, and the game will find a way, as it always does. To the students, it will feel as if the game had always been there. The game will make its demands. All they'll have to do is answer. And why wouldn't they? It's such fun. Such old fun, the oldest fun there is.

## ABOUT THE AUTHOR

**Natalia Theodoridou** has published over a hundred short stories, most of them dark and queer, in magazines such as *Strange Horizons, Uncanny, Beneath Ceaseless Skies, Nightmare,* and *F&SF,* among others. He won the 2018 World Fantasy Award for Short Fiction and has been a finalist for the Nebula Award in the Novelette and Game Writing categories. Natalia holds a PhD in Media and Cultural Studies from SOAS, University of London, and is a Clarion West graduate. He was born in Greece, with roots in Georgia, Russia, and Turkey.

# Futuristic Fruits and How Our Real World Seems Science Fictional Sometimes (in a good way!)

D.A. XIAOLIN SPIRES

There's a scene in the original *Firefly* TV series that sticks out to me and probably many others—the infamous strawberry scene from the intended pilot episode, "Serenity." What is this precious cargo the crew has been schlepping around, besides (*spoiler alert*) the nutritional/medicinal bars and a mysterious stowaway? Why, a fruit, thanks for asking. Kaylee Frye opens a small wooden box from Shepherd Book and pulls out a single strawberry. There may be more strawberries in there, but probably not many, given the box's size. She pulls out just one—large, juicy, gleaming crimson, seated firmly in her two fingers as her lips wait poised, examining it, an exquisite, lush rarity in the harsh arena of space and space delivery. She bites.

Now, some say that when you have a child you see the world in a new light. I do, I think! And when I see my child bite into a strawberry as large as her tiny palm, I can't help thinking of that scene. With the juices running down her chin and the utter enjoyment on her face, I have a flashback to Kaylee's patient examination of the strawberry's achene-studded physique, her anticipation for the bite, her teeth digging into the flesh and the growing smile thereafter.

It also makes me think, wow, we live in a world of plenty (not to downplay of course the growing crises of climate change, entailed aridification and flooding, and other quite serious environmental challenges). Environmental issues and ecological threat are precisely so stark because we only have one Earth. And this Earth produces amazing things. Compared to the starkness of space with even the world beyond the EVA suit trying to kill us, a strawberry seems such a luscious treat, sweet with a mélange of undertone flavors, a miracle of thousands of years of human traditional breeding, some of its varieties now patented and sold under only one brand. (I'm talking about you, Driscoll's.)

I don't always live in awe, walking through the supermarkets with my hand over my mouth gasping. Yes, there are fruits. Yes, they look gorgeous, impeccable, without flaws. It's become a mundane thing. We toss it into our carts, roll away without a second thought except to think what aisle next, whittling down our shopping list. But, thinking about it, sometimes our real world seems science fictional. How do we have such succulent, mouthwatering treats? And such an abundance of it? ( . . . at least in some parts of the world.)

The answer lies within a combination of landscape, environment, human ingenuity and our ability to transform the world around us with agricultural technology and plant breeding, and advances in distribution and shipping, climate control and refrigeration in general, as well as the whole invention of the modern supermarket itself. On the surface it seems quite magical.

We live in a world where you can roll in and roll out with whole pineapples, guavas, pomelos and grapes—and fruits galore out of season. Some of this is about trade routes and have and have-nots, some of this is about research and development, and much of this is the resourcefulness of the human enterprising mind, its aspirations, and our insatiable appetites for fructose-tinted sweetness.

Science fiction abounds with fruit and conceptions of what fruit means. Let me start from an arm's reach away, low-hanging fruit, so to speak: mythology and mythological and religious cosmology. There are many examples of fruit in speculative and adjacent fiction, often appearing in mythology, folklore and fairy tales.

There is the Tree of Knowledge in the Garden of Eden. In Norse mythology, goddess Iðunn keeps apples that are imbued with immortality and once consumed, they preserve youth. In India, mangos and coconuts are rife with meanings of auspiciousness and purity and used in puja and felicitous ceremonies such as weddings. Iconic in the savannah, the Baobab tree (which is a succulent) according to legend, is said to once comprise of the center of Senegalese villages, with the buoye "monkey fruit" juice providing necessary nutrients.

Fruit is also involved in acts of self-sacrifice and kindness, such as 'Kū, Hawaiian god of farming and fishing turning into 'ulu breadfruit as a way to nourish his family. Xiantao peaches confer immortality to the Eight Immortals of Chinese mythology. There are boys and peaches:

Momotarō who was born from a peach, and (though not mythological per se, but certainly a story time staple and folkloric in its telling) Roald Dahl's family favorite, *James and the Giant Peach.*

Fruit can sometimes be healing and wondrous, but also dangerous. Snow White lures and tempts with a poisoned apple. The Assiniboine tribe's trickster eats berries which induce him to scratch until he bleeds. "Bayabas," the guava in Filipino legend, was transformed from a greedy King Barabas into a fruit for the people by a hungry beggar denied of rations. The lesson: if you're not kind, considerate, generous, you might be turned into a fruit.

There are legends galore to expound upon these fruits, and their respective astounding properties and journeys.

Moving away from myth and more into futuristic speculation, there are also some science fiction works that bring up fictional futures of fruits and their interaction with parameters such as the divine and profane, fake and real.

Isabel Yap's "Milagroso" touches on this subject of miracle fruits. Her story contrasts two kinds of fruit (as well as produce in general): the more-delicious-than-nature fruit grown in greenhouses to the miraculous and hard-to-come-by "real" fruit given to a select house by San Isidro in a Lucban festival.

"Milagroso" challenges us to consider how we categorize these fruits by asking: what is divine, what is profane, what is natural and what is artificial? Is the true miracle and the food worth revering, the fake foods of recent human production and development that mimic real foods? (I suppose a corollary in our real world might be artificial flavoring or genetically modified organisms (GMO) crops.) Or is the real miracle in this futuristic Philippines fruits of "natural" production, i.e. a "real" fruit gifted by saints?

To be fair, "real" fruit requires inputs, fertilizer and dirt, and can beget pests such as bugs and rot. (Though some real fruit IRL is also grown in greenhouses, which is arguably, an environment of some artifice.) Fake fruits seem to sanitize this affair, maybe produced in lab conditions, without these inputs, perhaps printed or cell-cultured (i.e. vat-grown which sounds a lot less appealing), chock-full of nutrients designed into them.

Which one is the real miracle here? Are miracles invented? Are they naturally sprung? (And what does natural mean, anyway?) Are they strewn by a divine hand? Yap's story touches upon these subjects, 'real' fruit sprouting and transforming from the invented more artificial-like human-crafted (super-)fruit.

Bioengineered fruits ("genehacked" or "generipped") get limelight (pun intended!) in Paolo Bacigalupi's *The Windup Girl*, with featured fruits from Asia such as lychee, rambutan and durian.

The first chapter involves protagonist Anderson Lake acquiring a now-rare fruit, sniffing it, inhaling its volatile molecules, the aesthetic and sensory-rich descriptions making me as the reader heady with its smell and taste. The rambutan of this chapter also gets labeled with the word "miracle" and as "valuable" cargo as he carries it, with its "real flavor."

Bacigalupi's description makes the rambutan so appealing, an authentic-tasting fruit in a world where much of the produce tastes not quite as wonderful. This amazing rambutan, is reminiscent of a past that has long gone. (This is not to be confused with the use of rambutan in Netflix's *Another Life*, intended not to be the recognizable rambutan that it really was but as an "exotic" alien fruit on a "mysterious moon," much to the chagrin and hilarity of Southeast Asian viewers who encounter rambutan on a daily level.)

These stories of future produce tell of fruit as artifice and draws the metaphor of fruit as self, as connected to one's identity.

Among tables of meals including durian fruit that's "not quite right," Aliette de Bodard in "Immersion" also tackles fruit, embedding it in a virtual reality world. The immersed world is filled with avatars and the immerser generates distorted, transformed images of fruit and self by design.

There's also a commentary on colonization in terms of body image that could be discussed here (especially considering de Bodard paints a protagonist that views her stature through a jackfruit analogy and adjusts her avatar's skin color through the tech), and certainly there is an entire field of study that can be devoted to fruit as colonial objects, as being carried in freight trains and on ships across seas in our real world.

This academic research on fruit provides critical analysis on who labors to make the fruit, who gets to eat it, who owns the farms historically and currently, who owns the ships that carry them and who makes the big bucks.

Throughout human history, one only needs to look at: Haitian mangoes for export, pineapples as status symbols in Europe, "exotic fruit" oranges and bananas now mundane as still life captured in nineteenth-century paintings, the Banana Wars involving the U.S. in Latin America in the late 1800's to early 1900's, in colonial Taiwan exported to Japan in the 1900's, and how Latin American fruits became tossed on a wide-brimmed hat and marketed as Miss Chiquita, bringing about "exotic" and "other"-ing perceptions of gender and race as potent examples of fruit as fraught colonial objects, artifacts and concepts.

Political and economic disparities populate this real-life story. Yet in the story "Immersion," disparities are played out through fears and norms surrounding beauty. What is artifice? The food, including durian fruit, looks delicious but is "not quite right." Future fruit, through a virtual medium, as eerily "unreal" and is in juxtaposition of the layer underneath the virtual mask.

Stories such as these imagine a future stark without the lushness of real produce, real fruit, (of IRL today or yesteryear) and bring the readers back by offering such temptations from the past. There are notions of mimicry, nostalgia and yearning in these tales. Perhaps they can be interpreted as cautionary, as apprehension to yet-unknown or projected technologies of the plant-production present, but they also elucidate how much humans understand fruit as temptation, fruit as pleasure and fruit as oblation, fit for deities and bestowed upon us by the divine.

It also considers fruit as analogies for how we think of ourselves or real objects we consume that feed us and provide us with valuable nutrients, as well as fruit manifesting social and power dichotomies.

Since fruit is also how the English language talks about begetting and progeny, (e.g. fruit of my loins (and also the underwear that protects such valuables, e.g. Fruit of the Loom)), and is literally a part of a reproductive system in plants—entailed in its waxy skin and soft, edible flesh—fruit is conceptually and literally regeneration.

When I was writing my own story, "Seedless," I wanted to both emphasize and snip this parallel. I drew a connection between the breeding of seeds out of fruit (think: grapes and watermelon) and humanity's evolving forms of technology that increasingly disentangle and decouple the reproduction of our species from work situated in the body. Throughout history, fruit acts as both food nutrient-wise and a seed-bearing structure, with a new being waiting to germinate within.

This hasn't completely changed, despite new seedless varieties of fruit. Many fruits still have seeds: stone fruits (drupes) with pits, fleshy berries, pomes with their central cores mottled with seeds. The mythical apple, for example. Or the pomegranate, despite its name is a berry with arils, and its associations regarding life and death in Buddhist, Hindu and Islamic symbology. (Fun fact: the pomegranate botanically-speaking is not a pome, a fruit with a central core like an apple, but instead is a berry. The English word pomegranate comes from Middle English/ Old French pome meaning apple and the Latin word granatum [apple] and granum [seeds], so the etymology is deceptive, a language-based derivation rather than deriving from botanical classification.)

In present day, fruit continues to have seeds and seeds (unless genetically modified or selected otherwise) create life. This utilitarian view on seeds, distinguished by their botanical creative capabilities, is also why fruit is so pregnant with fertile metaphors: it literally carries within it the precursor to a new generation. And perhaps that's why it's so disturbing when the image of them is disturbed, warped in virtual reality or tainted by artifice.

And the latency, the potential for life, characterized by these fibrous and vitamin-packed orbs, is perhaps also why fruits seem so magical, so fragrant and juicy, a miracle in our hands, so fecund and ripe with meaning.

## ABOUT THE AUTHOR

**D.A. Xiaolin Spires** steps into portals and reappears in sites such as Hawai'i, NY, various parts of Asia and elsewhere, with her keyboard appendage attached. Her work appears in publications such as *Clarkesworld, Analog, Nature, Terraform, Fireside, Star*Line, Liquid Imagination,* and anthologies such as *Make Shift, Ride the Star Wind, Sharp and Sugar Tooth, Deep Signal,* and *Battling in All Her Finery.* Select stories can be read in German, Spanish, Vietnamese, Estonian, French and Japanese translation.

# Love and Care: A Conversation with Sofia Samatar

ARLEY SORG

Sofia Samatar was born in Indiana. Her father is from Somalia, and her mother is a Mennonite from North Dakota. "My parents were both teachers, huge readers, and passionate about foreign languages." Samatar's father was a professor of African history who wrote and edited books and journals, and her mother taught English to speakers of other languages. "Although I didn't always feel sure about going into teaching, it was in the air at my house. Eventually I decided that teaching literature was the best way to pursue my goal of turning my life into a giant book club."

Samatar attended a Mennonite high school and went to Goshen College in Indiana—also a Mennonite institution. She earned her master's at the University of Wisconsin-Madison, studying African languages and literature. Afterwards, she married writer Keith Miller. They lived in Sudan (now South Sudan) for three years and Egypt for nine years, teaching English. Samatar then studied Arabic literature in Madison, earning her PhD.

Samatar has also lived in Tanzania, London, New Jersey, and Pennsylvania. More recently, she moved to Virginia, where she teaches African literature, Arabic literature, and speculative fiction at James Madison University—she is a Roop Distinguished Professor of English. "The Shenandoah Valley is beautiful, but it was really my bestie who drew me here. Later, I fell in love with both the place and my job."

In 2012 Sofia Samatar had three short stories published, including "Honey Bear" in *Clarkesworld*. That same year, Small Beer Press published her debut novel, *A Stranger in Olondria*, which won a William L. Crawford Fantasy Award, a British Fantasy Award, and a World Fantasy Award. Samatar also received the 2014 Astounding Award for Best New Writer. *Olondria* was included in *Time*'s 100 Best Fantasy Books of All Time and *Esquire*'s 50 Best Fantasy Books of All Time. Samatar continued to publish well-received short fiction over the next few years, including notable "Selkie Stories are for Losers" (*Strange Horizons*, January 7, 2013) which was a BSFA, Nebula, World Fantasy, and Hugo finalist.

*Olondria* follow-up *The Winged Histories* came out with Small Beer in 2016, to critical acclaim, and was a Locus Award Finalist; and collection *Tender* (Small Beer, 2017) was a Locus, BFA, and World Fantasy finalist. Collection *Monster Portraits*, illustrated by Del Samatar and published in 2018 by Rose Metal Press, may have made less of a splash in genre circles (besides a BSFA finalist spot for Best Artwork) but received serious praise from venues like *L.A. Review of Books*, *Chicago Review of Books*, was listed as one of NPR's Best Books of 2018, and was a finalist for the Calvino Prize.

Likewise, 2022 memoir *The White Mosque* seems to be absent from some of the genre lists and databases but won a Winner of the Bernard J. Brommel Award, was a finalist for the Pen/Jean Stein Book Award (which awards the winner $75,000), received heaps of praise from place like *Los Angeles Times* and *Library Journal*, and landed on lists such as the New York Public Library Best Books of 2022. *Tone*, "a collaborative study of literary tone" co-authored with Kate Zambreno came out from Columbia University Press in 2023 and her latest work, fiction title *The Practice, the Horizon, and the Chain*, is due from Tordotcom Publishing later this month.

***Did you do any kinds of writing workshops, like Clarion West or Odyssey?***

I didn't do writing workshops, except for two intensive poetry workshops of one week each when I was in college. Our teacher was the poet Nick Lindsay, who passed away a few years ago, and he was amazing. He would bellow lines of poetry at random, jump up and down, and suddenly grab and attack a guitar or recorder (it was not clear that he could play either, but he made a lot of noise). Then he'd make arcane pronouncements like "When I am broken on the rack of life, from that arises my life's work!" Nobody had any idea what was going on. I adored him.

***Who do you see as your literary influences or heroes, and what do you like most about their work?***

Tayeb Salih is a major influence on me—I wrote my dissertation on his work, and have taught his novel *Season of Migration to the North* several times. That book includes many elements I love: tangled timelines, multiple voices, stream-of-consciousness passages, references to literature and mythology, descriptions of weather and light. These are all things I find in the work of my favorite modernists, James Joyce and Virginia Woolf, as well as beloved contemporary writers like Kate Zambreno, Carole Maso, and Bhanu Kapil.

I'm also influenced by fantasists who dance on the edge of reality: Jorge Luis Borges, Carmen Maria Machado, Jeff VanderMeer, Kelly Link.

***Do you see any of these influences show up in specific ways in The Practice, the Horizon, and the Chain?***

I think they must all be there, at some level, but the most prominent works in my mind were the Bible and the novels of William Faulkner. *The Practice, the Horizon, and the Chain* is about the persistence of myths: even in the far-future setting, my characters are in thrall to ancient stories about power and hierarchy, as well as enduring dreams of liberation. I happened to be reading a lot of Faulkner (I was trying to figure out how the same person could have written a novel as bad as *Soldier's Pay* and then, just three years later, *The Sound and the Fury*), and I was struck by the rhythms and overtones of his language that seem to flow right out of a Black church service. It seemed to say a lot about how writers imbibe language, intentionally or not. I wanted to direct that flow of sound and imagery into a story that's very different from Faulkner's work, a utopian story.

***I've read in prior interviews that writing and editing A Stranger in Olondria took more than a decade. What was the journey like for The Practice, the Horizon, and the Chain, from inspiration to publication?***

I am pleased and relieved to say that it did not take nearly as long! The direct inspiration for the book was a virtual conference at Boston College called Building the Fugitive Academy, where I listened to lots of brilliant, radical scholars discuss the work of transforming institutions and imagining new worlds. I attended that conference in 2021, wrote the book that year, revised it over a couple of years, and that was it.

***This new work features "the boy" and "the woman" --which some reviewers call "nameless characters." What were your intentions, why "the boy" and "the woman" instead of a more conventional naming system?***

This choice stems from the situation on the ship where these characters live. There are three distinct classes of people, and only those at the top use names. It's not only the woman and the boy who lack names in the story—all kinds of people from the middle and lowest classes are unnamed. They're referred to as guards, workers, students, elders, and so on.

Of course, being unnamed is not the same thing as being nameless. I'll leave that part for readers to explore.

***The boy is reluctant to leave behind familiar circumstances, even if those circumstances are terrible, which is a little different from what we often see in stories. Can you talk a bit about this narrative decision, what it means and why it's important?***

The boy comes from a place at the bottom of the ship, which is called the Hold. People there live in chains. This is powerful imagery in a U.S. context, an unmistakable reference to the Middle Passage and the history of enslavement. So yes, the boy's circumstances are terrible, but my story emphasizes the fact that even under these conditions, there is love and care. The boy has friends, a community, a mentor who shelters and teaches him. When he's taken out of the Hold to go to college, it's an improvement in his material circumstances, but emotionally, it's shattering.

***What are your favorite things about these two characters, what is important to know about them?***

The boy is an artist and a dreamer. The woman is a scholar, a college professor, and very tired! She has dreams too, but she's exhausted. My favorite thing about them is the way they manage to carve out space for genuine study, which is worldbuilding, in an institution that's fundamentally hostile. They're creative. They're willing to be naïve, to propose changes that seem outrageous, to ask *Why not?*

***One of the many things I've seen people praise about this book is your prose, including descriptions and details. Craft-wise, what is the key to writing great prose?***

That is lovely to hear, and I wish I had a good answer! If I had a formula or technique, I'd use it, but I don't. The only thing I have is reading. I recommend getting drunk on words. Read, read, read until you can't help writing. Then write.

***What is important to you about The Practice, the Horizon, and the Chain? When you think about the story as a whole, what is central to what you are setting out to do?***

This book is for everybody who likes speculative fiction. But in a particular way, it's for people connected to large institutions, especially universities, who feel discouraged about the inequities that persist in those places, even with many people working themselves to the bone to create change. When I wrote the story, I had the idea of a small book you could tuck in your bag and carry into some terrible institutional meeting, the kind of meeting that frustrates you and wastes your time and does nothing, and you'd put your hand on this book and think—*yes. Somebody sees me. Somebody knows.* And it would be as if you were surrounded by a glow. That's why the story needed to have a wild, fantastical element. It had to be a bit of a romp. It's for people who need a break.

***Besides your acclaimed novel-length work, you are also well-known for short fiction and poetry. Do your experiences writing at one length impact or change your approach to another? Does writing poetry influence your longer works?***

I don't consider myself a poet, though I've dabbled, and I love poetry—I read some every day. I'm awed by the depth of the relationship poets have to language. I do think there's something wonderful about writing shorter forms, because it allows you to grasp the structure of a work. Writing short stories has heightened my sensitivity to the shape of a piece, even a longer one—its overall design.

***If readers were to look at a couple of your short stories, what would you most like them to see, and why?***

I'd like them to sense a variety of voices. I think of the short story as a laboratory, a place to try things out. I'd like readers to feel that shifting, experimental quality—the difference between the lush, romantic atmosphere of a story like "Wolf Tones" and the more formal, mock-academic tone of "Fairy Tales for Robots."

***What else are you working on, what's new or coming up that you'd like folks to know about?***

I have a nonfiction book coming out in August. It's called *Opacities: On Writing and the Writing Life*, and it's a series of meditations on writing, publishing, and friendship.

## ABOUT THE AUTHOR

**Arley Sorg** is an associate agent at kt literary. He is a two-time World Fantasy Award Finalist and a two-time Locus Award Finalist for his work as co-Editor-in-Chief at *Fantasy Magazine*. Arley is also a SFWA Solstice Award Recipient, a Space Cowboy Award Recipient, and a finalist for two Ignyte Awards. Arley is senior editor at *Locus*, associate editor at both *Lightspeed* & *Nightmare*, a columnist for *The Magazine of Fantasy and Science Fiction* and an interviewer for *Clarkesworld*. He is a guest critiquer for the 2023 Odyssey Workshop, and is the week five instructor for the 2023 6-week Clarion West Workshop, among other teaching and speaking engagements.

# Science Fiction Is Spice: A Conversation with Ann Leckie

ARLEY SORG

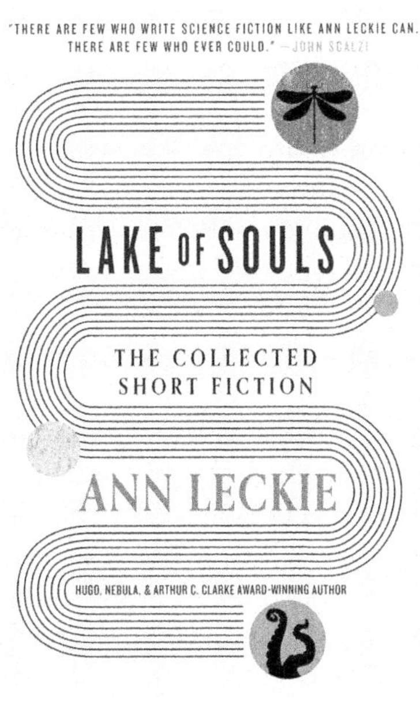

Ann Leckie was born in Toledo, OH and grew up in St. Louis, MO. Her parents gave her books to read but initially thought she'd "grow out of" science fiction. "I did benefit from living in easy walking distance from the local library, and I spent nearly every Saturday morning there through a lot of my childhood. It was wonderful to have that easy access to so many books. Libraries are the best."

Leckie earned a BA in music at Washington University. She also joined internet critique groups Critters and the Online Writing Workshop and participated in NaNoWriMo (National Novel Writing Month). In 2005 Leckie attended the Clarion West six-week writing workshop, where she wrote her first published SF story, "Hesperia and Glory" (*Subterranean Magazine* #4, 2006). The story was reprinted in *Science Fiction: The Best of the Year, 2007* (edited by Rich Horton for Prime Books). Leckie would sell numerous short stories—some of which were selected for various year's bests—before the 2013 publication of landmark title *Ancillary Justice*.

"I was working as a lunch lady when I sold *Ancillary Justice*. It wasn't a full-time job—at the time, in fact, I was only an Emergency Backup Lunch Lady, because I'd decided I really needed to focus on getting *AJ* finished and out the door. I wasn't supporting the family with my income, so that made it easier for me." Debut novel *Ancillary Justice*, published by Orbit, swept major genre awards: British Science Fiction Association, British Fantasy Association, Kitschies, Locus, Nebula, Clarke, and Hugo—it even won a Seiun Award; not to mention placing for a few other awards as well. *AJ* began the Imperial Radch series, which includes 2014 title *Ancillary Sword* (Hugo and Nebula Award finalist and BSFA and Locus Award winner) and 2015 title *Ancillary Mercy* (Hugo Award, Nebula, and Dragon Award finalist with a Locus Award win). She added novel *Provenance* to the universe in 2017, which garnered BSFA, Locus, Hugo, and Seiun nominations. She also added *Translation State* in 2023, to multiple starred reviews and a Dragon Award nomination.

In 2019 Orbit published Ann Leckie's *The Raven Tower*, a novel in a world for which she had already written and published several short stories. *Raven* earned her Dragon, Locus, and World Fantasy nominations, as well as a Hugo nomination which she declined.

Ann Leckie has worked as a waitress, a receptionist, a rodman on a land-surveying crew, and a recording engineer. "It's difficult to resist picking up a new hobby, or cycling through them, so I'll be in a knitting phase, or a beading phase, or a metalwork phase, or whatever. Currently I'm on a sewing jag, and it's pretty amazing to be able to make clothes that actually fit!"

Leckie lives in St. Louis with her family. Her latest is collection *Lake of Souls*—with stories "From the Imperial Radch Universe," "From the Universe of The Raven Tower," and an untitled section—due from Orbit this month.

***What, for you, does science fiction and fantasy do which is perhaps different from other forms of fiction?***

I'm not honestly sure. Sometimes I think it's just a question of, like, spice in food—a story strikes me as bland if it doesn't have some kind of odd worldbuilding or strange tech. Like, when I'm very tired or need some kind of light reading, I will happily pick up one of the fluffier sort of romances (not all romances, obviously, are fluffy or light reading) but it really has to be either historical or have some fantastic element.

Which isn't to say I don't absolutely love a lot of amazing realist works. Just, if given a choice, I'd rather have spec in there somewhere.

To a certain extent, having a long history of reading SFF has made me familiar with the ways SFF constructs worlds and interrogates things and so it just feels comfortable. But I do think SFF does different things or can do certain things more easily—it's great for being able to look at contemporary things from very different angles, and getting perspectives that you wouldn't ordinarily get. Of course, it doesn't always do that, sometimes it's just about blowing up spaceships or whatever, which is absolutely fine in my opinion.

I really do feel that a great popcorn book that's just sheer fluffy fun is deserving of tremendous respect -sometimes I think people kind of sniff at the idea of a book that's "just" escapist entertainment or consider it an insulting thing to say about a book or an author, but that's such an important thing to be able to have, and it's by no means easy to write. (I want to add, too, that it's important to have different *kinds* of escapist entertainment, because different people are escaping different things about the real world and entertained by different things. We should have all the flavors of popcorn and cotton candy!)

***You founded and edited magazine GigaNotoSaurus for several years. "A little bigger than Tyrannosaurus, a little smaller than Spinosaurus," the magazine is a venue for stories of novelette and novella length. How did editing the webzine come about, and what impact, if any, did it have on your own fiction?***

Before I wrote *Ancillary Justice*, I was trying to write short fiction. And finding that I naturally was writing fairly long works—things over ten thousand words. And most of the publications I ran across weren't buying anything longer than about five thousand, and often even shorter—this was the heyday of online flash fiction, actually. So I set out to learn to write shorter and shorter.

But I often wished that there were more places that would take longer work. And when I inherited a small chunk of money I decided that I could do a very simple online magazine, so I did.

If nothing else, editing *GNS* gave me a feel for what was working in a given story and what wasn't working, and why. After you read that much slush, with an eye to whether you can make it work or fix the things that aren't working for you, and how that might be done—I feel like I got much better at doing that with my own work.

***Long before the publication of* Ancillary Justice*, you attended Clarion West in 2005, and quickly sold your first short story (written at Clarion West) to* Subterranean Magazine*. What is your relationship to short fiction, how does it compare to your relationship with novels?***

I have a somewhat fraught relationship with short fiction! Left to my own devices I'm going to write a novel, or at least a novelette. (Oddly I don't think I've ever produced a novella!)

I had a weird experience when I tried writing shorter and shorter, I finally got down to a three-hundred-word piece (which is in the collection actually) and I figured that was as low as I was going to get and focused on turning out stuff at about five thousand. And then I sat down to do *AJ* and I felt this sense of panic—I chose a starting place as far in as I possibly could, and I still had so much exposition to fit in and I couldn't possibly do it. And then I realized that this was not, in fact, a short story and I had as much room as I wanted, and I realized how different the habit of writing short fiction was from novels.

***Lake of Souls* *brings together eighteen of your stories, divided into three sections. Do you see this as a "best-of" or is there another organizational drive at work? And were there pieces that were considered which didn't make the final cut?***

There are a few pieces that didn't make the final cut. One, "The Long Game," because it only came out in 2023. A few because they're very early works that I don't think stand up. But there aren't many of those, and this collection is more or less complete.

***What can you tell us about original "Lake of Souls" without spoiling the read too much?***

"Lake of Souls" started as a speculative biology idea my daughter suggested to me, a particular kind of genetic parasitism that, while we walked the dog, we worked up into something we thought was cool and interesting. It was such an interesting idea that with her permission I made a story around it.

***The oldest publication date in Lake of Souls is that first short story, "Hesperia and Glory," while the latest (besides the original piece) is "The Justified," originally published in 2019 anthology The Mythic Dream. Looking at this body of work as a writing journey, what has changed about your craft, your approach, or your interests, and the way they come through in your fiction?***

I've definitely become more confident. Looking back, there are a lot of deliberate structural choices that I made so that I would know where to even begin, which is a thing that causes anxiety in a lot of aspiring writers. These days it's not as though I don't plan a structure in advance but it's generally not so strict or so, I don't know, overt? I guess it's like riding a bike—at first it's awkward and you're thinking about every move very consciously, and then after a while you just do it.

***When you think on these stories, are there underlying themes or motifs that run through many of them, concerns you often come back to and speak to in your fiction?***

I honestly don't know. I suspect it's much easier for other people to see than me.

***Publishers Weekly praises your "detailed worlds, intelligent plotting, and clear-eyed compassion . . . " What is the key to great plotting, especially in the confines of shorter fiction?***

It seems to me that it's the confines of short fiction that are the biggest factor in plotting it—you can have as large and elaborate a plot (and world) as you like, but you've only got a certain amount of space to fit it all into. So you have to slice off whatever won't fit, and either imply it or do without it.

I also feel that good plotting isn't just following traditional forms—not that a writer can ever totally escape traditional plots, they're the air we breathe basically and there are plot shapes that readers come to expect and that our minds just produce without even thinking about it. But it's important to question those expectations when you see yourself reproducing them. Is that really what you want to say? Is that really what your characters would do? Thinking of the characters as people, as though they were real people, not stereotypes, or dolls you're moving around. Plot is very much the result of character, just as characters are a product of their world.

(I've got nothing against moving dolls around and telling stories, I spent a lot of my childhood with an assortment of paper dolls who lived in a town made of cardboard boxes and had all kinds of drama, much of which I don't even remember now.)

***If readers were to look at three stories in this book, what would you most want them to read, and why?***

Hmm. "Lake of Souls," certainly, because it's new. The others—it's difficult to say! It would depend so much on which reader and what I thought they would like best or what they might want the most out of a story.

***You commented in a recent interview with Locus Magazine that "Nobody paid much attention to my stories." The publication of Ancillary Justice was met with a heap of awards. Did the recognition and attention create a sense of pressure, did it motivate you to write more, did it change your perspectives on the industry?***

It was a very, very strange experience. To go from publishing but only a few people seemed to have read my work to what seemed like the whole SFF world knowing my name—it was just bizarre and hallucinatory. It was exhilarating and also terrifying, because it wasn't just a few short fiction readers seeing the work, it was seemingly everyone.

At first it made writing a lot more fraught—so many people were expecting more work from me and highly interested in what it would be! It was terrifying. But after a while it actually got easier, and now sitting down to a new piece doesn't inspire the anxiety it used to. After such a large sample of reactions to my work, it's clear to me that some people will like it and some won't and that's just how things are, so I'm writing for the people who will like it.

When I first started out, I was desperate to sell my work and I would have written whatever in any sort of way that might get an editor to cut me a check and publish my words. I kept looking for whatever that one thing would be—"The Endangered Camp," in fact, is a product of my having seen an interview with John Joseph Adams—who was reading slush for *F&SF* at the time—where he said that he wished he would see more stories in slush about dinosaurs, or about space elevators, more post-apocalyptic stories, or stories about Mars. And I was trying to sell to *F&SF* and hoping JJA would pass my stories up to Gordon, and I thought "Well, the dinosaurs had an apocalypse, how do I involve Mars or a space elevator?" I didn't get the space elevator in.

I'm happy with how that story turned out, actually. But one of the things I've learned is that working too hard to please some theoretical editorial taste isn't going to help you much in the long term. I mean, unless you're a genius at doing that, which I'm sure some people are. But these days I'm going to focus on what interests me in a project, and not what I think an editor will like. And when I tell writers that—I taught at Clarion West a few years ago, and just a few months ago I taught at the first Wandering Wormhole, a bunch of fabulous young writers—I often get skepticism in return. And I remember that my perspective now is very, very different.

***What else are you working on, what's coming up that readers should know about?***

Currently I'm working on a draft of my next novel, which doesn't have a title yet, but is set in the Imperial Radch universe.

## ABOUT THE AUTHOR

**Arley Sorg** is an associate agent at kt literary. He is a two-time World Fantasy Award Finalist and a two-time Locus Award Finalist for his work as co-Editor-in-Chief at *Fantasy Magazine*. Arley is also a SFWA Solstice Award Recipient, a Space Cowboy Award Recipient, and a finalist for two Ignyte Awards. Arley is senior editor at *Locus*, associate editor at both *Lightspeed* & *Nightmare*, a columnist for *The Magazine of Fantasy and Science Fiction* and an interviewer for *Clarkesworld*. He is a guest critiquer for the 2023 Odyssey Workshop, and is the week five instructor for the 2023 6-week Clarion West Workshop, among other teaching and speaking engagements.

# Editor's Desk: An Alternate Reality

## NEIL CLARKE

This month presents an unusual situation. I'm actually writing two editorials and if you are seeing this one, things either turned out better than we expected or we've somehow earned a momentary reprieve. I had originally put the odds of this path at around one-in-ten. The other editorial may still be necessary, so perhaps that wasn't wasted time. I certainly won't complain if you never see it. (Sorry to be cryptic, but not saying what the other one was about may be necessary.) In any event, publishing this version is a good thing.

In keeping with the good news vibe that has presented itself, I'd like to turn this into an opportunity to recognize some of the recent award news from some of our authors.

The following stories have been included in the annual 2023 Locus Recommended Reading List:

- "To Sail Beyond the Botnet" by Suzanne Palmer, novella
- "Such Is My Idea of Happiness" by David Goodman, novelette
- "An Ode to Stardust" by R.P. Sand, novelette
- "Thin Ice" by Kemi Ashing-Giwa short, short story
- "Window Boy" by Thomas Ha, short story
- "Day Ten Thousand" by Isabel J. Kim, short story
- "Zeta-Epsilon" by Isabel J. Kim, short story
- "Pinocchio Photography" by Angela Liu, short story
- "Stones" by Nnedi Okorafor, short story
- "Bird-Girl Builds a Machine" by Hannah Yang, short story

The Nebula Awards, presented by the members of the Science Fiction and Fantasy Writers Association (SFWA), has placed three of our stories on their 2023 ballot:

- Best Novelette: "Imagine: Purple-Haired Girl Shooting Down The Moon" by Angela Liu
- Best Short Story: "Window Boy" by Thomas Ha
- Best Short Story: "Better Living Through Algorithms" by Naomi Kritzer

The British Science Fiction Association has announced this year's BSFA Award finalists and we're very excited to see Fiona Moore in the Best Short Fiction category for "The Spoil Heap."

The Canberra Speculative Fiction Guild announced their 2023 Aurealis Award finalists and quite happily, Thoraiya Dyer's "Eight or Die" is up for Best Novella.

And by now, the Glasgow Worldcon has announced the Hugo Award finalists. It's possible I've missed someone (because not everyone tells their editor and this issue had to be put to bed before the official announcement) but it appears we have two stories on the ballot. "Introduction to 2181 Overture, Second Edition" by Gu Shi, translated Emily Jin is a finalist for Best Novelette and  "Better Living Through Algorithms" by Naomi Kritzer is up for Best Short Story I'm also quite pleased to say that I'm once again a Hugo Finalist for Best Editor Short Form! Thank you to everyone that nominated me!

Congratulations and best of luck to all our finalists! We really appreciate the love and support shown to them and hope you continue to find works you enjoy enough to celebrate within our pages.

## ABOUT THE AUTHOR

**Neil Clarke** is the editor of *Clarkesworld Magazine, Forever Magazine,* and several anthologies, including the Best Science Fiction of the Year series. He is a eleven-time finalist and the 2022/2023 winner of the Hugo Award for Best Editor (Short Form), has won the Chesley Award for Best Art Director three times, and received the Kate Wilhelm Solstice Award from SFWA in 2019. His latest anthology, *Best Science Fiction of the Year: Volume 7,* is now available from Night Shade Books. He currently lives in NJ with his wife and two sons.

# Hermit Crab Walker

## COVER ART BY LONGQUE CHEN

## ABOUT THE ARTIST

**Longque Chen** has over seven years of experience working in the game industry and is currently employed by Striking Distance Studio as senior concept artist. He graduated from Central Academy of Fine Arts and earned his BFA from Art Center College of Design. His works are focused on science fiction designs like mecha, robotic stuff, props, weapons, and vehicles.

Printed in Great Britain
by Amazon

41531072R00088